WILMOT AND POPS

Also by Alex Shearer

Wilmot and Chips

For older readers

The Crush

WILMOT AND POPS

Alex Shearer

a division of Hodder Headline plc

First published in Great Britain
by Hodder Children's Books in 1998

10 9 8 7 6 5 4 3 2 1

A Catalogue record for this book is available from
the British Library

ISBN 0 340 71641 X

Typeset by Avon Dataset Ltd, Bidford-on-Avon, Warks

Printed and bound in Great Britain by
Mackays of Chatham plc, Chatham, Kent

Hodder Children's Books
A division of Hodder Headline PLC
338 Euston Road
London NW1 3BH

Wilmot and Pops

"You," said Terry, "are a big liar."

"And you," said Wilmot, "are a big fat fibber. And when I'm Number One in the charts and have millions of people all screaming for me and buying my record and wanting to be my friend and when I've got millions of pounds in my piggy bank and you're still a big nobody with a crummy biscuit tin – you'll be sorry. You'll be so eaten up with jealousy, there'll be none of you left."

"You!" Terry jeered. Number one in the charts! Don't make me laugh. What charts are they, Wilmot? The Spotty Dingbat Charts? Because you'll be Number One in them all right, no trouble at all."

"You'll see, Terry," Wilmot said. "You'll see. I'll be big pop star, I will . . ."

Contents

1

Boo-Jitsu

The sound of that week's Number One in the charts came to an end in a blaze of guitars.

"And don't forget," the DJ reminded his listeners, "to tune in next week. Same time, same place, same spot on the dial for the Official Chart Countdown. All the best selling records, right here on your favourite radio station. And now, after the commercial break—"

Wilmot Tanner reached out and turned off the radio. He'd had enough commercial breaks to last him a lifetime. Not that he'd lived that long. It just seemed that way sometimes. He looked across at his brother Terry, who had his nose stuck into a Superman comic.

"You know, I reckon I could be a pop star, Terry," Wilmot said. His brother looked over at him and raised an eyebrow in scorn.

"You?" he said in disbelief. "A star? You'd have trouble even being a twinkle."

"I could!" Wilmot confirmed. "I could be a rapper or something."

"What? A chocolate bar wrapper? No, I don't think so, Wilmot. You couldn't even be a crisp bag."

"I could," Wilmot said, more taken with the notion every second. "I could be a pop star. A huge pop star. An enormous one. A mega-star. Not just a star, a black hole even."

Terry stared at him again.

"You?" he said. "Be a pop star. You can't play anything. You couldn't even get a note out of an envelope – not unless it was a sick note, of course."

"Yes, I could," Wilmot said. "In fact I can almost play the piano by ear."

"Yeah, can't play it with your fingers though, can you?" Terry said. "You're tone deaf, you are, Wilmot. They wouldn't even have you in the school choir. You sound like somebody sandpapering his wooden leg. You sound like a frog with a frog in his throat. In fact you sound like a frog with a toad up his nose and a couple of tadpoles in his ear. That's what you sound like."

"I know more about music than *you* do," Wilmot said, starting to get a little bit niggled with his brother.

"What do you know about music?" Terry jeered. "You don't even know how to work the CD player. That's how musical you are."

"Yes, I do!" Wilmot said. "I know everything about music. And at least I can play the recorder – a bit."

"Oh, a *bit*, yeah. Can't play *all* of it though, can you? The only bit of the recorder you're any good with is cleaning it with the duster."

"Well, what have you ever got a tune out of come to that, Terry?" Wilmot demanded. "Apart from your bottom. The only time a tune ever came out of your mouth was when you accidentally spat out your cough sweet."

"I can play the drums," Terry said, and, as if to prove it, beat out a rat-a-tat-tat with the palms of his hands on Wilmot's head.

"My head," Wilmot said, "is not a drum."

"It's pretty similar though, isn't it, Wilmot. It's hollow and empty and hasn't got anything inside it, has it?"

"Yeah, well your leg's a xylophone then," Wilmot said, giving Terry's leg a decent whack with the letter knife. "Besides, you haven't even got proper drums – just a couple of old biscuit tins. And as for your drumsticks, they're just a couple of old biros. I've seen chickens with better drumsticks than you."

"So?" Terry demanded. "So what? Beethoven started off with a couple of old biscuit tins as a matter of fact. And so did the Beatles. And loads of other great musicians. In fact Beethoven wrote a whole sympathy for nothing *but* biscuit tins – it's called 'Beethoven's Biscuit Tin Shortbread Sonata', in A Sharp Pencil. And they have them in the Caribbean too, steel bands, all playing biscuit tins."

"That's oil drums, not biscuit tins," Wilmot said.

"They may be oil drums but they keep biscuits in them to stop the flies getting at them. So don't show your ignorance, Wilmot. Fat lot you know about it. I mean, you can't even read music, can you?"

"I can look at the pictures," Wilmot said.

"There aren't any pictures!"

"I can imagine them. Anyway, I bet I could be a pop star," Wilmot said again, as if repeating it might make it come true.

"No, I doubt it," Terry said. "I mean, it's not just the music, Wilmot, it's the rest of it too. Because pop stars are supposed to be good-looking, aren't they?"

"So?" Wilmot demanded. "What's that supposed to mean?"

"Well, there you are then," Terry said. "Haven't got much of a chance, have you, not with a face like that. You could never be a heart-throb."

"Yes, I could, I'm dead handsome, I am."

"You are not. You'd be lucky to get a job as a doorknob, Wilmot. You've got a face like a pine cone. It's no wonder the mirror runs away and hides behind the shower curtains when it sees you come into the bathroom."

"Well what about you?" Wilmot said. "They ought to pass a law saying you have to wear a paper bag on your head so as not to frighten little babies and nervous cats."

"I'm going to get you for that, Wilmot," Terry said. " 'Cause I'm learning Boo-Jitsu after school, see. And I've learned how to kill with just one squeeze of my thumb."

Wilmot looked at Terry suspiciously.

"What do you mean, Boo-Jitsu?" he said. "I've never heard of Boo-Jitsu. You mean Jujitsu, don't you?."

"No. It's like Jujitsu," Terry said, "only Boo-Jitsu is more of a surprise."

"Well, in that case," Wilmot said, "I've been learning Karate Fingers of Steel during my lunch hour, and I can floor a fifteen-stone bully just like that, with one finger. I only have to stick my finger up his nose and twist it in a special way and say the magic Japanese words, and he's a dead man."

"What magic Japanese words?" Terry said warily.

Wilmot thought a moment.

"Rice crackers," he said. "Only I say it in Japanese. But I can't say it now as I'm only allowed to say it when I attack people. So don't even bother asking me to say it in Japanese right now as I wouldn't want to kill anyone by accident."

"You," said Terry, "are a big liar."

"And you," said Wilmot, "are a big fat fibber. And when I'm Number One in the charts and have millions of people all screaming for me and buying my record and wanting to be my friend and when I've got millions of pounds in my piggy bank and you're still a big nobody with a crummy biscuit tin – you'll be sorry. You'll be so eaten up with jealousy, there'll be none of you left."

"You!" Terry jeered. "Number One in the charts! Don't make me laugh. What charts are they, Wilmot? The Spotty Dingbat Charts? Because you'll be Number One in them all right, no trouble at all."

"You'll see, Terry," Wilmot said. "You'll see. I'll be

a big pop star, I will. People will want my autograph—"

"You'd better learn how to spell your name then," Terry advised him. "Only one y in idiot, remember."

"And I'll have girls chasing me in the street—" Wilmot went on.

"Make a change from dogs then," Terry said.

"Yeah, thousands of them," Wilmot dreamed, "all wanting to tear my clothes off."

"What you mean so as they can wash them because your socks are so smelly?"

"And I'll make millions of pounds from big recording deals. And I'll drive around in a big stretch limo with its own TV and a fridge full of ice cream in the back and a football pitch in the boot. But don't worry, Terry, I won't forget you when I'm a pop star, even if you still are a big nobody. I'll let you be my roadie, that's what I'll do. I'll let you carry my guitar around for me and let you clean my blue suede shoes for me every night – with your tongue—"

Terry got hold of Wilmot round the neck with a special Boo-Jitsu hold.

"Listen, Wilmot," he said, "if you're not careful, I'll make you eat your blue suede shoes. I'll make you swallow them whole without even chewing them. And then I'll make you have the laces for afters."

"You don't frighten me, Terry," Wilmost said. "And if you don't let go of my neck I'll say the special Japanese word for rice crackers and destroy you with my little finger."

Now Terry knew that Wilmot was bluffing. He knew that Wilmot didn't know how to kill a man with his finger and that he didn't know the Japanese words for rice crackers. But he released him just the same. No sense in taking unnecessary chances after all.

"Well just you keep a civil tongue in your gob then," Terry said rudely, "or I'll get you with a Boo-Jitsu Surprise. And as for you ever being a pop star, Wilmot, well, you've more hope of getting to the moon in a rowing boat."

"As a matter of fact," Wilmot said, "I have been to the moon in several rowing boats. Loads of times. I go there quite regular. I just don't happen to boast about it, that's all. Not like some big-mouthed brothers I could mention, who never stop going on about themselves because that's the only person they ever think of."

"That's it, Wilmot," Terry said. "You've done it now. You've pushed me too far. I'm going to Boo-Jitsu you now. You're going to find out what pain really means."

"And you're going to find out what a Karate Finger of Steel up the nose really means," Wilmot said.

And a moment later the two of them were rolling around on the living room floor like a couple of squabbling cats. They banged into the coffee table and sent it flying and the ornaments on it crashed to the ground.

Their mother, Mrs Tanner, came rushing in from the kitchen.

"Terry, Wilmot!" she yelled. "Stop that at once! You're fighting again."

"No, we're not," Wilmot said, trying to get his finger out of Terry's nose. "We were just looking for something. Terry lost his Walkman and I thought it might be up his nostril."

"That's right," Terry said, letting go of Wilmot's ear, which he seemed to be twisting off. "We were just tidying up and I thought Wilmot would look a lot tidier with his ears on round the other way."

Mrs Tanner looked at the mess on the floor and at the upturned table.

"Pick that lot up, please, and I mean *properly*, and then go to your rooms. And if there's any more fighting for the rest of the day, any at *all* – then no pocket money for a week."

"But Mum," Wilmot protested as he righted the table. "It's been no pocket money for a week for ages. In fact, I worked it out last night that we're not entitled to any pocket money now until the year 2078."

"Well you'd better behave then, hadn't you?" Mrs Tanner said. "Now go up to your rooms and read quietly for a while."

Once they had put everything back where it belonged, Terry and Wilmot slunk from the living room and headed upstairs.

"It's all your fault, Wilmot," Terry said under his breath, accidentally bumping into him on purpose as they got to the landing. "In fact, I'm going to get you for that, Wilmot, because I'm learning Korean Smack boxing after school – which is like Kick boxing only there's more smacking in it – and I'm going to smack your head off, see."

"You'd better not try it, Terry," Wilmot warned

him, as he inadvertently trod on Terry's foot, mistaking it for a woodlouse, "because I've got a special SAS combat manual in my room, and I know how to kill a man in two seconds with the inside of an old toilet roll. So watch it."

With a final "accidental" nudge in the ribs, Terry went into his room, slamming the door behind him. Wilmot stood outside Terry's door a moment, pulling faces and making rude signs.

"I can see you," Terry's voice came through the keyhole.

"Don't care if you can," Wilmot said. "You're still a stupid Wally."

"And you're a daft nerd!" Terry said. "With knobs on. Very spotty knobs at that."

"No I'm not," Wilmot said, "and I'm going to be a pop star with a big Number One."

"Make a change from being a big number *two* like you usually are," Terry's voice said through the keyhole.

But Wilmot just ignored him. If Terry wanted to be stupid, that was his problem. Wilmot had bigger fish to fry. Who *was* Terry, after all? An accident of nature, a fluke who happened to be his brother. And what had he ever done anyway? Who was he to belittle the hopes and dreams of others? Just because he was a bit older, he seemed to reckon that he knew everything. But he didn't. Not by a long chalk. And Wilmot was going to show him. Yes, Wilmot was going to show them all. Just as soon as he was Number One in the charts.

2

A Cry for Help

As Wilmot lay on his bed staring up at the model spaceship which lazily revolved from a string taped to the ceiling, he thought deeply about his future in the recording industry and in the field of popular music.

The more he thought about it, the more attractive an idea it became. In fact he wondered why he hadn't done something about it all ages ago. In many ways it was the perfect answer to all his problems. Once he was an internationally known pop star with a big hit record at Number One in the singles charts and with a CD album to follow, he'd be made. You could earn millions from pop records, he knew that. He'd heard his dad say so, many times. They'd be sitting there watching Top of the Pops together and his dad would say things like, "Call that music? They get all that money for making a racket like that? That's not music, it sounds more like a crocodile choking on a set of bagpipes." (Wilmot didn't ask why a crocodile would be swallowing a set of bagpipes. He knew there would be no point.)

"It's an *awful* noise, isn't it, Wilmot?"

"Yes, Dad," Wilmot would say, to keep on the right side of him in the hope of him persuading their mum to change her mind about the pocket money. "Terrible racket." (But he quite liked the music really and had to make an effort not to tap his foot.)

"I mean, now look at that, Wilmot," his dad would say, whenever a particularly outrageous pop singer appeared on screen. "Look at that hair. Look at the way they're dressed. Is that a boy, or a girl? Or is it a chimpanzee?"

"Neither, Dad," Wilmot would say. "It's the Smurfs."

"Well, even if it is," his dad would go on, "they ought to know better. No, there hasn't been a decent group since the Beatles, if you ask me. Now they knew how to write a proper tune. How did it go again, that favourite of mine? Oh yes – dum-dee-dum-dee-dum. Now that's what I call real music – built to last."

But Wilmot would be concentrating hard on the TV screen, watching, looking, listening, taking it all in. Yes, if Wilmot could just get a number one in the charts, his problems would be over.

It all came down to money in the end, as things often do.

The way things were – what with his mum banning pocket money until the year 2078 – by the time Wilmot next got a pocket money instalment, he'd be an old age pensioner.

It was all Terry's fault too, because he'd started all the fights that had got the pocket money suspended in the first place. According to Wilmot's notebook, Terry had started forty-seven arguments all in the one day – and that was only up until lunchtime. After lunch he had then provoked another nineteen disagreements, eight serious punchups, plus two attempted murders and a suicide bid – all by three o'clock. It had been one of those rainy Sunday afternoons when there wasn't much else to do other than argue with your brother and drive your parents up the wall. And so they had. In fact if their mum had gone any further up the wall she'd have been swinging from the lampshade.

"Every time you two argue from now on," she'd finally told them, "I'm going to stop your pocket money for a week."

At that Wilmot and Terry had made a real effort to stop annoying each other, but somehow it hadn't worked. It was in their blood. By the following Saturday morning – according to their mum's calculations – they'd had over four thousand separate quarrels, brawls and arguments.

"Which means," she then concluded, putting down the calculator, "that there's no more pocket money until the year 2078."

They went a bit quiet at that. It was a long time to go without pocket money. Wilmot might even be dead before he got any more. And what use was pocket money when you were dead? What could he spend it on in heaven? Were there any sweet shops there? And what about Terry? What would he spend his pocket money on down in hell? Because that was where *he* was going, no doubt about it. He'd probably like it down there too. It was Terry's sort of place, hell. A bit like his room, probably. Sort of hot and sweaty and muggy and a touch smelly, like it was full of bad eggs.

But no pocket money until the year 2078! It was a life sentence. In fact it was probably illegal. His parents probably weren't allowed to do it. Wilmot even thought of getting the police on to them. But then, he reasoned, if he got his mum arrested he wouldn't get any tea. So he didn't bother. But all the same, the more Wilmot brooded over his loss of pocket money privileges, the more convinced he became that it was probably an illegal act on the part of his mother. In fact, it was probably classed as cruelty and neglect.

Looking at the school notice board one morning, he had spotted a poster up there which said: "*Do you have problems at home? Unhappy? Neglected? In despair? Can't talk to your parents? Need some friendly advice? Call KidScrape, the confidential help and advice line. Don't let it go on. Don't let a problem turn into a crisis. Ring us now.*"

Wilmot had made a note of the phone number and he had called it the instant he got back home.

"Hello," a pleasant lady's voice had answered. "KidScrape Advice and Help Line. Don't be afraid and don't hang up. We're here to listen and we're here to help. Take your time and say things in your own way. All calls are treated in strictest confidence. Now, how can we help?"

"Hello," Wilmot said, "it's Wilmot here. Wilmot Tanner."

"Hello, Wildot," the kindly lady said. "And what

can I do for you. Do you have problems at home?"

"I should say so," Wilmot told her. "It's absolutely horrendous."

"Are you being subjected to violence and cruelty, dear?" the lady asked, her voice full of concern.

"Not half," Wilmot said. "My brother's been at me with the Boo Jitsu again. But fortunately I know how to defend myself with my ancient Karate Finger of Steel. I only have to say rice crackers in Japanese and he backs off sideways."

There was a moment's silence at the other end of the phone.

"I see, dear," the lady said, but there was something in her tone which implied that she didn't quite see at all. "So you're not *actually* being hurt?"

"Oh no," Wilmot said. "At least nothing serious. And anyway, I know how to kill a man with the inside of an old toilet roll, so I'm not bothered myself. And even if I don't have an old toilet roll on me at any particular time, I could always use a sausage."

There was another silence at the end of the phone. A longish, sort of baffled silence.

"Are you still there?" Wilmot asked.

"Yes," the lady's voice said. "Only – I'm not quite sure what the problem is here, Wildnot—"

"Wilmot," Wilmot said, "not Wildnot,"

"No, dear, it's just what is the problem exactly, Wilbot? If it's not your brother, is it your parents?"

"Yeah," Wilmot said. "It is. That's it. It's my parents. That's it. You've got it."

"Are they cruel to you, dear, at all?" the lady asked, sounding more concerned than ever.

"Not half," Wilmot said. "All the time. Constantly – from the moment I wake up. Sometimes they even make me eat cabbage."

"So this cruelty – what form does it take – is it mental or physical?" the lady asked.

"It's all sorts," Wilmot said. "And it starts from first thing in the morning."

"Why, what happens then, dear?"

"They make me get out of bed," Wilmot said, "when I'm still tired. It's cruel. And that's not the half of it. You know what else they make me do?"

"What, dear?"

"They make me go to school!" Wilmot said.

"Oh, dear," the lady managed to say.

"Yeah," Wilmot agreed. "And it's not just now and again. It's day after day. It's been going on for years and I'm powerless to stop it. It's five days a week! On and on, with only a couple of months off in the summer. I mean, it's a bit steep, isn't it. Going to school one day every fortnight or so would be all right, but not all the time."

"But Wilgrot," the lady said. "Most children go to school five days a week."

"Maybe," Wilmot agreed. "That doesn't mean it's not cruelty, does it? But that's not what I wanted to talk to you about. It's far worse than that. It's what our mum's done to us. It's awful, it really is. I can hardly speak about it, it's so bad. I don't know where to turn or how to go on. I'm that desperate I don't know what I'm going to do. If things get any worse, I might even have to have a bar of chocolate."

"What has your mother done exactly, dear?"

"She's stopped our pocket money until the year 2078."

There was a very, very long silence at the end of the phone and then:

"I see," the lady said. "And that's it? That's your problem? You're not getting any pocket money? That's why you've called the KidScrape help line?"

"Yeah. I don't suppose you get problems as bad as this every day, eh?" Wilmot said.

"Well – but *why* has she stopped your pocket money, Wilbot?"

"Because me and my brother keep arguing. She says we're driving her round the bend."

"I see." There was another longish pause and then the lady asked, "And what exactly were you hoping we at the KidScrape Advice and Help Line could do about that, Wilbot?"

Wilmot took a deep breath and came straight to the point.

"I was wondering if you could send me a few quid just to tide me over until my pocket money starts again. I'm normally too proud to ask for charity, but things are sort of desperate. You don't have to send any to my brother Terry. Just me'll be fine."

The lady made a very long – exceptionally long – speech at this point, all about not wasting people's time and how some children in this world had *real* problems, not piffling imaginary and trivial ones, and that these genuine cases were probably trying to get through on the advice line right *now*, so would Wilmot please get off it so that those who needed real help could get through.

So the answer was basically no. KidScrape would not send Wilmot a few quid until his pocket money started again.

Wilmot put the phone down. He felt disappointed and let down.

"Typical," he thought. "They say they want to help poor suffering children who're going through bad times at home, but when it comes to putting their hands in their pockets, they won't even lend you a fiver. That's the trouble with these help lines. They're all talk."

Seeing that no money would be forthcoming from KidScrape, Wilmot then turned his attention to other means of raising cash. But he was too young to even buy a lottery ticket. In fact he was too young to do most of the things he wanted to. It seemed that his mind was too old for his body. He was too young to see the films he wanted to, too young to get a full-time job, too young to do anything interesting.

But he wasn't too young to be a pop star, was he? There was no law saying that you had to be over eighteen or something to have a Number One in the charts. Or if there was such a law, nobody had told Wilmot about it.

No, he was quite sure that the field was open to everyone. And he wouldn't even need pocket money then. Not when he was a million selling chart topper. He'd be giving pocket money to his mum (well, only if she and Dad didn't argue.) He might even buy her a gold-plated ironing board.

So yes, the more that Wilmot thought about it, the clearer it seemed that if only he could become a pop star, then his pocket money problems would be solved. Why, he might even throw a handful of fivers in Terry's direction, just for the pleasure of seeing him grovel to pick them up.

Of course he had a few things to do first – like get a group together, write a hit song, get it recorded and get it played on the radio. But all these things were details, really, mere details.

Wilmot had the master plan, the grand vision, that was the main thing. Once you had the plan, the rest would fall into place, as easy peasy as clockwork pie.

Wilmot went over to his bedside table. He picked up his comb and then he got a piece of tissue paper from inside the old shoe box where he used to keep his hamster. He found a cleanish strip of tissue paper, tore it off, and wrapped it around the comb. He blew and then sort of hummed a bit. A fairly pleasant sound came out. He tried again, a bit louder. Then he launched into a full rendition of. "The Flight of the Bumble Bee" as spontaneously arranged for comb and tissue paper by Wilmot Tanner himself.

The result sounded pretty good to Wilmot. So good that he didn't even hear Terry beating on the wall shouting, "Stop that horrible racket, Wilmot, before I go mad! You're making my ears bleed! My bed's having a heart attack!"

Even as he played, Wilmot pictured himself up on stage at some outdoor pop festival, like on the TV. He could see the thousands and thousands of fans stretched out before him, their hands held up in adulation, some of them carrying banners with We Love You Wilmot written on them or All We Need Is Wilmot. There were people passing out from the heat and the excitement. Wilmot's backing band was behind him on the stage, pumping out his latest Number One hit at high volume.

"We'd now like to play for you 'The Flight of the Techno Bumble Bee'," Wilmot was saying, and the crowd went wild. It was the moment that everyone had been waiting for – the highlight of the whole event – Wilmot's solo spot on comb and tissue paper. He blew for all he was worth and the crowd erupted into shouting, yelling and applause.

"Throw me your old tissue paper, Wilmot," his fans beseeched him. "Let me brush my hair with your comb, Wilmot," a voice from the front of the mob cried. "I haven't got nits or anything, honest."

"Shut that horrible row up!" another fan called . . .

Hang about. Reality was intruding into his dream. That was Terry again, banging on the wall that separated their rooms.

"Belt up, Wilmot!" Terry yelled through the wall. "Or I'll kidnap your stick insect."

Wilmot stopped playing. "You touch my stick insect, Terry," he yelled back, "and I'll do experiments on your rabbit – with electricity."

"You touch my—"

But then their mother's voice echoed up the stairs.

"I heard you two. You're fighting and arguing again. That's another week without pocket money!"

By Wilmot's calculations that now took them up to the year 2079. It was a long time to go without pocket money. A very long time indeed.

3

Comb and Tissue Paper

When he deemed it safe to do so, Wilmot tiptoed out of his room and headed for the stairs, his comb and tissue paper in hand. If he couldn't practise in his own room undisturbed, then he'd go and practise out in the garden.

He tried to sneak out unobserved, but his mother saw him.

"I thought I asked you to go to your room, Wilmot."

"I did. But you didn't say I couldn't come out again."

"True. So where are you off to now?"

"Just out into the garden," Wilmot said. "To look for something."

"For what?"

"Inspiration. To compose."

His mother gave him a quizzical look.

"Compose what?"

"A Number One hit," Wilmot said. "Excuse me."

And he went out of the back door, headed for the far end of the garden, opened up the shed door and sat down in the wheelbarrow.

Now Wilmot knew a *bit* about composing and writing songs. He knew that you had to have a bit at the beginning, then another bit, then a catchy sort of twiddly bit, then a chorus bit, then you went back to the beginning bit again, and then you did all the other bits, and then you had an end bit.

He decided to start with the end bit as that was probably the hardest.

"Once I know how to finish it," he thought, "I'll be almost there."

He sat in the wheelbarrow practising end bits on his comb and tissue paper. After about ten minutes, he reckoned he was on to something. It went dum-dum-da-dum-dum, dum-*dum*.

"Sounds all right to me," Wilmot thought. "I'll leave it at that for now. You don't want to overdo this composing lark or it can drive you mad. Just like that classical composer bloke, Vincent Van Mozart who went totally bonkers and cut his ear off with a pencil sharpener. Besides, if I get a move on, I might get milk and biscuits if I offer to help

Mum with the washing. A lot of composers did that – helped their mums with the washing to get some milk and biscuits."

Wilmot left the shed – feeling that he had put a good afternoon's work behind him – and headed on down the garden playing the end bit on his comb and tissue paper.

Little did he know that he was being observed by four separate sets of eyes. One pair belonged to Terry who was up in his bedroom watching Wilmot, thinking, "What is he doing now?" followed up by a second thought, "Whatever he is doing, how can I turn it to *my* advantage?"

Not that Terry actually *thought* this. He didn't need to think it at all. He more *lived* it. It was ingrained in his being. It was like a thought you had without thinking. A reflex. More like breathing than thinking at all.

The second pair of eyes belonged to Wilmot's mum. She watched him from the kitchen as he headed along the garden.

"Here he comes," she thought. "Casual as you please. 'Can I help you with the washing, Mum?' he'll say. And then it'll be 'Any chance of some refreshments?' "

And she looked across the kitchen towards the biscuit tin and she smiled – knowing that she'd give him the milk and biscuits all the same – in fact, she might even restore his and Terry's pocket money.

The third set of eyes belonged to a pigeon which flew off.

The fourth pair belonged to a much more dangerous creature altogether – Wilmot's neighbour, Mr Ronson.

Seeing Wilmot out in the shed, Mr Ronson had tiptoed out into his own garden, keeping low and out of sight under the fence so that Wilmot couldn't see him until the last moment. Then suddenly he straightened and sprang up. His head appeared over the fence, level with Wilmot, who was strolling down the path, humming at his comb and tissue paper, his mind filled with thoughts of milk and biscuits.

"Ah, Wilmot lad!" Mr Ronson said. "It's you! What a coincidence meeting you out here in the back. You did surprise me and take me unawares. You were the last person I expected to see out here. Not much to do, eh? Feeling at a loose end—"

"No, Mr Ronson, not at all—"

"Looking for someone to have a bit of a chat with, eh, Wilmot?"

"No, not really, Mr Ronson, I was more thinking of milk and biscuits—"

"And why not," Mr Ronson agreed. "A good long chat to work up an appetite for some milk and biscuits, what could be a better idea. Well, I'm a busy man, Wilmot, I've got a whole retirement to get on with, but I could spare you a couple of hours if you're lonely and desperate for conversation."

"But I'm not lonely," Wilmot said. "I've got loads of friends."

"Ah, too proud to admit it, eh? Well, I can understand that. But it's nothing to be ashamed of Wilmot, that you're all alone and nobody wants to talk to you."

"No, but—"

"Normally I'm far too busy to spend an afternoon chit-chatting over the garden fence, but as you're all on your ownsome—"

"But – biscuits – milk – I—" Wilmot began to garble, but he knew it was already too late. Mr Ronson had got him again. Mr Ronson; the man with the longest and most boring stories for miles. He had waylaid him and trapped him good and proper.

"So what's that you've got there, Wilmot? Comb

and paper, is it?" Mr Ronson asked.

"Yes, Mr Ronson," Wilmot said. "I've been composing. I'm going to be a pop star and have a Number One in the charts."

"Are you now?" Mr Ronson. "Well, that is interesting. Because I used to be quite a pop star myself as a matter of fact. Not under my own name, of course. I had a stage name back in those days. I was in a group known as Rocking Ronson and the Flim Flams. I was Rocking Ronson and the rest of them were the Flim Flams. We were bigger than the Beatles at one time – at least in Norway we were. We had several hit records over there. You might have heard them on the radio, Wilmot. 'Lonesome Reindeer Blues', that was one of ours and 'Someone's Pinched My Snow-shoes', that was another of our big hits. And 'We'll Meet Again, Sven, Round About Half Past Ten'. And 'I've Got My Left Ski On My Right Foot, Baby, So No Wonder I'm Going Sideways.' Only trouble was it got so cold over there in Norway that during one concert the song lyrics froze and we couldn't sing them, Wilmot, you see. And then the drummer's sticks got frozen to the skins. Yes, it was so cold during that concert that several walruses out in the fiord – who'd swum in to listen to the music – had to be given fishermen's pullovers by the coastguard to stop them from freezing to death. But there was nothing we couldn't play, Wilmot," Mr Ronson continued. "I'm a highly gifted, natural musician. In fact, you know what they say about gardeners having green fingers, well, I've got the musical equivalent of that."

"What's that Mr Ronson?"

"Green ears. But yes, I've got amazing natural gifts musically speaking, Wilmot. I can pick up any instrument you care to name."

"What about a church organ?" Wilmot asked.

"That might be a bit heavy," Mr Ronson admitted. "But usually I can get a note out of anything. Why, I even got a note out of the cash dispenser by the bank the other day – a ten pound note! Get it, Wilmot. That's a joke that is."

"Oh, is it, Mr Ronson? Thanks for explaining."

"Not at all, Wilmot. I know you're a bit slow on the uptake so I don't mind dotting the eyes and crossing the tees for you."

Wilmot looked murderously at him.

"Well, if you'll excuse me, Mr Ronson, I must—"

"Of course you must, Wilmot, but before you do, I'll just tell you the very interesting and highly educational story of how I toured the world once with a mate of mine called Timpani Hargreaves. We were off in search of the Lost Chord, you see, and the rumour was that this bloke had heard it somewhere up near the top of Mount Everest. So there the two of us were, scaling the heights of Everest, dressed in black tie and tails and carrying a grand piano – most of which Timpani Hargreaves had in his rucksack – when we met a yeti coming the other way. That's like an abominable snowman. So I said to him, 'Have you heard the Lost Chord?' And he said, 'Not yeti I haven't, but'—"

Wilmot's attention drifted. He let his thoughts wander away. Yes, he knew that the pop star idea was a good scheme, but he also knew that ambitions weren't enough on their own. They had to be realised. They had to be achieved. First some work had to be done. He needed a realistic strategy, a sound plan. And as soon as he could get away from Mr Ronson, he would make one. He'd write it all down formally, using pen and paper. He'd call it Wilmot's Plan for Stardom. Part One.

The sun was setting. Wilmot's dad was home. There was his mountain bike, parked by the kitchen door.

The window opened and his mum called out across the garden.

"Wilmot, don't keep Mr Ronson talking. You're always bothering the poor man. Time for tea. Come in and wash your hands, please."

Wilmot looked pleadingly at Mr Ronson. How long had he been going on now? Would he take the hint and stop? Would his battery ever run down?

"So we struggled home across the Himalayas, Wilmot, me and Timpani Hargreaves, with the injured abominable snowman lying on the grand piano with a bandage round his leg and the Lost Chord clutched to his bosom. But just as we were crossing a narrow rope bridge over a massive canyon, it gave way underneath us, and down they all fell, lost forever – apart from me, who managed to cling on to the leg of a passing vulture which carried me to safety in its nest, two hundred feet up in a tree. And for the next two years, I lived the life of a vulture, Wilmot. I couldn't let on I wasn't a vulture you see, or they'd have eaten me. So I used to keep the nest tidy and polish the eggs with me hanky. But that's another story."

"And is it as big a pack of lies as this one, Mr Ronson?" Wilmot asked.

"I beg your pardon, Wilmot?" Mr Ronson said tetchily, replenishing the tobacco in his pipe.

"I said I think I can hear my mum calling. I'd better go in."

"Off you go then, Wilmot." Mr Ronson said. "Better not keep your mum waiting. Nice to talk to you."

"Nice to listen to you, Mr Ronson."

Wilmot went in to tea.

"It's a shame for that lad," Mr Ronson thought. "He's quite a personable sort of chap really. I wonder why he seems to have no friends of his own. He always seems desperate for a chat. Always comes out into the garden whenever he sees I'm here. Oh well. If I can help somebody. That's the main thing."

As Wilmot pushed open the kitchen door, he took a last look behind him to see Mr Ronson stuffing tobacco into his pipe. The tobacco was as bad as his compost heap. It was hard to know which of them smelt worse.

It was a form of cruelty having a neighbour like Mr Ronson, Wilmot thought. A form of cruelty to children. Maybe Wilmot should ring up the Kid-Scrape help line about him. Perhaps he could get some proper counselling. Or even a bit of pocket money.

4

Kipper Song

While they all sat eating their tea, Terry looked across from his slice of pizza to Wilmot on the other side of the table. A strand of cheese, almost as thin as a spider's web was hanging from Wilmot's mouth. Terry nearly told him about it, but decided that it might be better not to say anything and be more fun to watch it get stuck to his chin instead.

Terry chewed his own pizza slice with deliberation. It was this new scheme of Wilmot's that was bothering him. Wilmot was always having schemes – sort of the same way the cat kept getting fleas. Mostly – like the cat fleas – Wilmot's schemes were no more than a minor irritation to the household which would soon go away given proper treatment. And the proper treatment was usually to let Wilmot get on with it and for him to find out the error of his ways.

"He's a bit headstrong, is Wilmot," Terry thought – and not for the first time. "He's not one to look before he leaps. Which is why he's always landing in trouble. Must be."

Not that Terry minded Wilmot landing in trouble. It was fine by him. He could land in as much trouble as he wanted. Just as long as Terry wasn't in there with him.

But this latest scheme was bothering Terry. His instincts told him that this number one in the charts business was yet another of Wilmot's over-ambitious – not to say totally stupid ideas – which was all going to end in tears.

And yet – and yet – and yet—

What if Wilmot was right?

No.

Terry squinted at Wilmot, narrowing his eyes. Just say by some awful fluke that Wilmot *did* have a number one in the charts? And Terry wasn't part of it. He had no share of the action. Just imagine Wilmot getting all that money and spending it all on stupid, wasteful and unnecessary items – like himself.

Yes.

Maybe Terry ought to bide his time, and keep an eye on how things developed. He was sure in his heart that there was no way Wilmot could ever make it as a pop star, not when the only musical instrument he could really play was the comb and tissue paper. But all the same, he'd have to watch him. Because you never knew with Wilmot. You never really knew at all.

"You're both very quiet," Mrs Tanner said.

"Very quiet," Mr Tanner agreed. "Very quiet indeed. No arguing at all tonight."

"Yes, in fact you're both behaving so well," Mrs Tanner announced, "I'm going to restore ten years worth of pocket money."

"Oh great," said Wilmot. "That means we'll only have to wait until the year 2069 to get some. Things are looking up. Great, eh, Terry?"

"Yeah," grunted Terry. "Marvellous. That's really cheered me up that has."

But he didn't sound as if he meant it.

After tea Wilmot went up to his room to do some more work on his Number One chart hit. He couldn't seem to get much beyond the end bit though, and although there was nothing actually wrong with *dum dum dee-dum dum, dum-dum* he couldn't see it topping the charts somehow. At least not for long. In fact, Wilmot did wonder if he hadn't heard dum dum de dum dum, dum *dum*! somewhere else before, and if maybe he'd borrowed it by accident. Things like that often happened, copying other people's tunes by mistake.

Realising that he was not going to get much further with the song on his own, Wilmot decided it might be best to have a collaborator – someone he could bounce ideas off. Unfortunately, there was only Terry immediately available, so with some reluctance Wilmot went along the corridor and tapped on his door.

"Hello, Terry," he said, trying to sound as friendly as possible.

"What do you want, banana-face?" Terry demanded, looking up from his football manual, "apart from your head squashed by a road-roller that is."

"Oh ha ha, very funny, very good Terry, ha ha," Wilmot said, not rising to the bait. "No, I just wondered if you were any good at song writing."

"I should think so," Terry said. "I'm good at most things."

"It's just I'm a bit stuck on my Number One hit and I wondered if you'd like to write it with me."

"Might do," Terry said, non-committally, seeing a chance to participate in Wilmot's potential success. "Of course, I'd want half the money in that case."

"What money?"

"Royalties. Every time your song's played on the radio you get money for it called royalties. I'd need half of that if I'd written half the song."

"Okay, Ter," Wilmot said. "That sounds fair enough."

"Okay then," Terry said. "What have you got so far?"

"Shall I sing it to you?" Wilmot offered.

"If you must."

"Right. Well, what I've got so far is the end bit and that goes *dum dum dee-dum dum – dum-dum!*"

Terry looked at him, his face blank.

"That's not a song!"

"It is," protested Wilmot, "it's the end bit."

"What about the rest?"

"I'm working on that. That's what I need the help with."

"Okay," Terry said, "but first, you're going to have to sign this contract." And he quickly scribbled something out on a piece of paper. "There."

"What's it say?" Wilmot asked.

"It says 'I give Terry at least half of everything I ever earn from being a pop star if not more, signed Wilmot.' And then you put your name there. In fact it's a sort of song-writing contract, Wilmot."

"Oh?'

"Yeah, and of course you'll need a manager if you get to be famous. In fact, I'd better draw up a management contract as well."

"Okay."

Terry quickly scribbled on another piece of paper and passed it over to Wilmot. It read, "I promise to give Terry at least half of my half of what's left of my money from being a pop star when I've given him the other half. In return for this Terry will bear full responsibility for all jurisprudence and for supplying sufficient biros for Wilmot to sign contracts with."

"Put your mark there, Wilmot," Terry said. "If you can't remember how to spell your name, just write Stupid, everyone'll know it's you."

"I'm not stupid," Wilmot said. "And I'm certainly not daft enough to sign this. Why have I got to give you half of *my* half when you're getting half already? And who's this Gerry Prudence anyway?"

"It's because it's like that in contracts," Terry explained. "It's all to do with 'heretofore' and 'notwithstanding'. They have a lot of that in the law. And it's all down to you being something called the party of the first part, whereas me, I'm the party of the second part. They generally have two parts, you see, Wilmot, in contracts, because that way it's easier to staple the pages together."

"I don't know—" Wilmot said. "Maybe I should get Dad to take a look at this."

"Don't bother him," Terry said. "Hasn't he got enough on his plate? Just sign the contract, Wilmot, come on. You're so suspicious you are. You have to learn to trust people."

Wilmot took up the pen, yet still he hesitated.

"But if I give you half the money and then half of my half, Ter, what am I left with?"

"Oh, loads," Terry said. "I wouldn't worry about that. The bit you're left with you'll be able to use to pay your income tax."

"Oh, all right." Wilmot said doubtfully. "Okay, I suppose so. I mean, you wouldn't deliberately swindle me, would you, Terry?"

"Please, Wilmot," Terry sighed, with a hurt look in his eyes. "Amn't I your brother?"

And so against his better judgement Wilmot signed the two contracts (although he did keep his left hand behind his back with his fingers crossed while he was doing so, just to be on the safe side.)

"Right," Terry said, once it was done. "Let's get on with this song then. Now, I reckon we should write the words first – the lyrics – and then a tune might come to us naturally. Now what'll we write about?"

Wilmot thought a moment.

"I know," he said. "Let's write a song about kippers."

Terry stared at him.

"Wilmot," he said. "You can't write Number One songs about kippers. Don't you ever listen to the songs on the radio? It's all about boy meets girl."

"What you mean like boy meets girl and then they have a fight?"

"No," Terry said. "Boy meets girl and then they have a snog."

"I'm not doing that!" Wilmot protested. "Snogging girls. I've got my health and reputation to consider. I'd have no friends left at school at all if I went round doing things like that, snogging stupid girls and stuff. Be reasonable, Terry. You can go too far."

"No, no!" Terry said. "You don't have to *do* it, you

only have to *write* about it. That's what the public wants to hear. Love songs, only with an original slant, sort of quirky."

"Well," Wilmot said, "how about – instead of boy meets girl – we have boy meets kipper? Or even girl meets kipper. Yeah, how would that be, Terry? That would be different. We could have a song about this girl falling in love with a kipper, only when she sticks a fork in it, it goes '*Ouch!*' So she realises it's still alive. So she kisses it then and it turns into a handsome prince. Prince Herringbone, the King of the Kippers. And then they get married and live happily ever after and open a smoked haddock factory."

Terry sat in silence a while, chewing thoughtfully at his lower lip. He looked at his younger brother with a serious frown.

"To be perfectly honest, Wilmot," he said, "I don't really know if you're cut out for song-writing."

"Well, it was only a suggestion," Wilmot said, a hurt look in his eyes.

"Yeah, I know that," Terry said, "and I'm not saying it's a bad suggestion, I just don't know how it would go down with the record buying public. It'd be different if kippers bought records. It would be a big hit no trouble at all then."

"They don't though."

"No."

"Well you suggest something then."

"Okay," said Terry, "give me a moment." He chewed thoughtfully at the end of his pencil and then wrote down a few lines. "How about this?" And he sang the following lines:

"I love you baby. Don't mean maybe. Gimme five. Snakes alive. Gimme ten. Now and then. Oooeee, oooeee. I'm so free. Feel like a cup of tea. Don't be late. You're my milkshake. Pass me the football. Let me buy you a burger, baby, down at McDonald's. And you can pay for the cokes."

There was a long silence while Terry waited for Wilmot's reaction. He seemed to be somewhat stunned.

"That, Terry—" he began to say, "that is absolute—"

"Yeah?"

"Absolutely fantastic. That's like poetry, Terry. I didn't know you could write stuff like that."

"Me neither," Terry admitted. "It just seemed to pour out of me. It was almost as if the pencil was writing it all on its own. Now how about a chorus then?" he added. "You need to have a catchy chorus, Wilmot if you want to have a number one hit. Something that'll stay in people's minds."

They both thought a moment. Then Wilmot snapped his fingers.

"Got it, Terry!" he cried. "Got it! How about this: Cadgy wadgy woo woo, cadgy wadgy foo foo. Cadgy wadgy choo choo. Oh baby if I had to choose between you and my trainers it would be a penalty shootout."

Terry seemed puzzled.

"Yeah—" he said, "yeah, I like the cadgy wadgy bit, Wilmot, I just don't get that last part about the trainers and the penalty shootout. I don't quite understand—"

"You know," Wilmot said. "It's love, Terry, like you said, all about love. And this bloke loves this girl so much that he loves her as much as his trainers. And so, if he had to give one of them up – his trainers or the girl – he'd have a hard job deciding. So, you know, it would be like a penalty shootout. Sudden death like."

"Ah, right," Terry nodded. "Yeah. I get you. I think."

He plainly wasn't too keen on the last line of the

chorus, but as he seemed unable to come up with anything better just then, it went down on the lyric sheet.

"Just the music now then," Terry said. "Now, what was the end bit you had again?"

"*Dum dum dee-dum dum, dum-dum!*" Wilmot reminded him.

"Right," Terry said, "in that case, for the rest of it, why don't we have: *Dee-dee dum dee-dee, crinka crinka chink! Boodle oodle crumchuck, winka poo a dink! Stinky winky wagalum, coochy winky scoot. Stinkaboo a ding-along hunkalumpa ingy pong, wingy scrump a toot!*"

"Yeah, great!" Wilmot said enthusiastically. "It'll be a Number One. Definitely, Terry, it really will. It's that catchy you just can't resist it. Everyone'll be singing it. All whistling it and dancing to it and everything. We're going to be pop stars, Terry. We'll be able to behave really badly and be indulged by the media and throw tellies and trouser-presses out of hotel bedrooms, and maybe even the beds too, if we can lift them. It'll be great."

"Okay," Terry said. "From the top then, let's give the whole thing a run through."

So, sharing the lyric sheet, and to the tune of *dum dum dee-dum dum* and so on, the two brothers sang out as loudly as they could, going through both lyrics and chorus.

"I love you baby. Don't mean maybe. Gimme five. Snakes alive. Gimme ten. Now and then. Oooeee, oooeee. I'm so free. Feel like a cup of tea. Don't be late. You're my milkshake. Pass me the football. Let me buy you a burger, baby, down at McDonald's. And you can pay for the cokes. Cadgy wadgy woo woo. Cadgy wadgy foo foo. Cadgy wadgy choo choo. Oh baby if I had to choose between you and my trainers it would be a penalty shootout."

As they sang, there was a clatter from down in the kitchen as Rufus the cat ran out of the cat-flap and tore down to the end of the garden. Then, when they had finished, there was the sound of Mrs Tanner thumping on the kitchen ceiling with a broom handle.

"That must be Mum," Wilmot said to Terry. "Telling us she likes it."

"Reckon so," Terry said. "I wonder what Dad thought of it. Where is Dad?"

Wilmot looked out into the garden. His father was out there on the lawn. He was wearing a pair of yellow ear-defenders, the kind worn by workmen on the roads when they are using road drills.

"He's out in the garden," Wilmot said. "He's got his ear defenders on for some reason too. Must be going to use the hedge trimmer."

"Probably," Terry agreed. "But I think we've got a Number One here, Wilmot."

"I think we definitely have," Wilmot agreed. "It'll be top of the charts in no time, it really will." He looked down into the garden again, and saw that Mr Ronson was out by his compost heap, staring up at their window.

"I wonder what Mr Ronson thought of it," Wilmot wondered. "He seems impressed. But why's he got that cotton wool in his ears."

But Mr Ronson didn't stay in the garden long. He hurried off down to the precinct, hoping to catch the chemist's shop before it closed.

"Have you got anything for earache?" he asked the pharmacist behind the counter.

"Is it mild or painful, sir?" the pharmacist asked.

"Painful," Mr Ronson said. "Very. Excruciating."

"Is it maybe an infection, sir?"

"No," Mr Ronson said. "It's the neighbours."

5

Marmalade Head

As he walked to school the next day it occurred to Wilmot that he was going to find it very difficult to play the comb and tissue paper and sing at the same time. He just didn't have enough mouth for it. Nor enough lungs either. And even if he could count on Terry to play the drums (well, the biscuit tins) that still wasn't enough to solve the problem. He was going to have to recruit a few more backing musicians. There was no way around it. It obviously meant splitting the money with somebody else, but that couldn't be helped. Half of something was better than all of nothing – that was the way to look at things, as Terry always said.

Terry had gone off with his mate Dave. Terry tried not to associate with Wilmot during school hours. It was an embarrassment for him to be seen with a younger brother and Wilmot felt pretty much the same about Terry too. So during school time they did their utmost not to be related.

Wilmot met his friend Martin just outside school and they walked across the playground together.

"Hey, Martin," Wilmot said, as they headed for their classroom. "You play the guitar a bit, don't you?"

Martin had an old guitar at home, and for a while he had even taken lessons until one of the strings had snapped and his teacher had suffered a nervous breakdown.

"Yeah," Martin agreed. "I'm still one string short mind, but it doesn't make much difference. In fact, my mum says I can make more noise with five strings than most people can with six. Why?"

"Well," Wilmot said, "the reason I'm asking is I'm thinking of becoming a pop star and being a big heart-throb and stuff and of having a Number One hit record and making millions of pounds and being dead famous and getting on the TV and having my photo in the paper and riding round in big white limos and having bodyguards to take me to school and stuff and throwing tellies out of hotel windows, and maybe even the beds, if I can lift them. But I don't know if you'd be interested in that, because I don't suppose it's everyone's cup of tea. I suppose some people would rather go down to the park and have an hour on their roller boots."

"Well," Martin said, hanging his coat up on its peg and not wanting to sound too keen, "I suppose I could give it a go. That is millions of pounds *each* we're talking about is it, Wilmot?"

"I should think so," Wilmot nodded casually, "Could even be squillions. I can't guarantee anything of course, it's a cut throat business, pop music. But I've got this great song that's a definite Number One, called 'Cadgy Wadgy Woo Woo'. Here, I'll sing it to you—"

But just as Wilmot was clearing his throat, Mr Phelps walked into the classroom and he had to save his demonstration for later.

Meanwhile, in another classroom, Terry Tanner was showing his friend Dave – whose dad was a solicitor – the contracts he had got Wilmot to sign. Dave read them through carefully then he handed them back to Terry.

"Water tight," he said. "Beautiful contracts. A model of their kind."

"I've got him then, have I?" Terry asked.

"Definitely," Dave agreed. "According to that contract, for every penny Wilmot earns, he's got to give you two. Or, to put it another way, if he earns fifty pence, then he has to give you a pound. The more he earns, the more he owes you. He'll be in debt till his dying day."

"So it's a pretty fair contract then?" Terry said.

"Oh yes," Dave agreed, "at least it is from your point of view, Terry. I don't quite know how Wilmot would feel about it. I don't suppose he realises what he's signed."

"Wilmot?" said Terry. "No, I shouldn't think so. He's got very limited understanding has Wilmot. He's more like one of your four-footed furry friends than anything. A sort of dumb animal, you know."

"Doesn't he know his rights then?" Dave asked.

"No," Terry said, "I don't think he knows he's got any. And I want to keep it that way."

After school that day, when Wilmot got home he asked his mum if it would be all right for Martin to bring his five stringed guitar round later.

"What for?" Mrs Tanner asked suspiciously.

"We thought we'd have a jam session," Wilmot said.

She looked at him even more suspiciously.

"Jam and what session?" she said. "Bread and jam?"

"No, Mum, not jam to eat – you know, musical jam, like when you make it up as you go along. We're getting a band together, and we're going to be pop stars, you see, and have Number Ones and that and buy mansions in the country and throw snooker tables out of hotel windows and tell everybody not to take drugs."

"But I didn't think you played anything, Wilmot," Mrs Tanner said. "You gave up the piano lessons, remember? And the flute lessons. And the trumpet lessons – though I was quite pleased about that. So what do you play in this band?"

"I'm more vocals," Wilmot said modestly. "Vocals and comb and tissue paper. And I might stretch to a tambourine at a push, or maybe shake a bag of crisps, that's very good for percussion that is. In fact, can I have a bag of crisps to shake, Mum?"

"Only if you promise not to eat them."

"Okay. So can Martin come over?"

"Well where are you going to practise? I don't want you making a noise in the house. Terry's got some homework to do – or is he in the band as well?"

Terry looked up from the kitchen table where he was busy writing a short essay – the shortest one he could manage – on the Saxon invasion.

"I'm more on the management side," he said. "I might help them out on the drums and biscuit tins occasionally, but I'm more responsible for handling the finance and negotiating the recording deals."

Mrs Tanner looked from her elder to her younger son and back.

"We'll practise down in the shed if that's all right," Wilmot offered.

"Well – I suppose so. If Martin's mum says it's okay."

"I'll ring him now," Wilmot said. "And get him to ask her."

So he did, and it was all right, and immediately after tea Martin turned up at Wilmot's back door, his guitar in his hand.

"There's good news and there's bad news, Wilmot," he said.

"Gimme the bad news first," Wilmot told him.

"I've broken another guitar string."

Wilmot groaned.

"And the good news?"

"My mum says I still make more noise with four

strings than most people do with six."

"That's all right then," Wilmot said. "Come on, the rehearsal studio's down at the end of the garden."

"I thought you only had a shed at the bottom of the garden."

"That's right," Wilmot said. "But it's been renamed."

So Martin took his guitar (with the two strings missing) Wilmot brought his comb and paper and his bag of crisps (for percussion only – to be shaken but not eaten) and they headed for the shed.

"I'll be down in a while to hear how you're progressing," Terry shouted after them as they went out of the door. "See if you're ready for the public yet – or if the public's ready for you," he added under his breath.

Martin and Wilmot made themselves comfortable on upturned flowerpots in the shed. Wilmot showed Martin the lyrics of the song he and Terry had written and he ran through the tune for him.

"Great lyrics, Wilmot," Martin said when he had finished. "The cadgy woo woo bit's dead catchy and I especially liked that part about the penalty shootouts."

"I wrote that," Wilmot said. "I think I must have been a bit inspired."

"Yeah. Only – what does the whole song really *mean*, Wilmot?"

"Well," Wilmot said, "no one really knows for sure. It's like poetry, see. It doesn't really mean anything. Or rather, it means what you want it to mean. Shall we run it through then?"

"Okay."

"A one a two a one two three—"

Martin struck a chord on his four stringed guitar and Wilmot had just launched into the first part of the song, "*I love you baby. Don't mean maybe. Gimme five. Snakes alive. Gimme ten. Now and then. Oooeee, oooeee. I'm so free. Feel like a cup of tea—*" when a loud hammering was heard on the back of the shed and a girl's voice boomed out.

"Wilmot Tanner! What are you doing in there? Are you torturing cats or what? I'll have the Royal Prevention on to you!"

Martin's strumming died on his guitar.

"What was that!" he said.

Wilmot swallowed hard.

"It's a girl," he said. "It's Amber. The neighbour."

"Amber who?" Martin said aghast. "I didn't know you had a girl living next door."

"We do now," Wilmot said. "Amber Watts her name is. She moved in a week ago. She goes to that girls' school up by the park where they all learn how to be Prime Minister."

"She can't half shout," Martin said. "Can't you do something about her?"

"It's not that easy," Wilmot began, "you see—"

There was another thump on the shed and Amber Watt's voice boomed out again.

"Wilmot Tanner come out of there and prove to me that you're not torturing dumb animals or I'll call the RSPCA."

"Won't be a minute, Martin," Wilmot said. "I'll soon get rid of her."

"It's all right," Martin said, "I'll come with you. I want to see what she looks like."

Wilmot led the way out of the shed and around the side. There, peering over the fence, were two girls. One was tall and formidable, with red hair and freckles, the other was smaller, and more mousy with a face which looked as if it had a permanent case of mumps.

There was no need to ask which of the two girls was Amber, that was perfectly obvious. But who, Martin wondered was the other one.

"That's her friend," Wilmot explained. "Silent Edith."

"Why's she called Silent Edith?" Martin asked.

"Because she never says anything," Wilmot explained.

"It's a good name then," Martin said. "Only why does she never say anything? Can't she speak?"

"No. She can speak when she wants to, she just doesn't want to."

"Very unusual that is," Martin said. "Not speaking like that."

"It certainly is for a girl," Wilmot agreed. "Normally they never shut up. It's not getting them to speak that's usually the problem, it's getting them to stop."

"Wilmot Tanner," Amber Watts demanded, leaning so far over the fence that she practically fell into Wilmot's garden, "what are you doing in that shed. I hope you're not torturing things."

"Don't be daft," Wilmot said. "We're having a band practice."

"Yeah, that's right," Martin agreed. "It's not

hamsters we're torturing, it's eardrums."

"Have you got a band then? That's interesting, isn't it Edith?"

Silent Edith nodded her agreement.

"Yeah, we're going to be pop stars," Wilmot said casually, "and make loads of money and be on the telly and be heart throbs and be dead cool and throw beds out of the window – if we can lift them – aren't we, Martin?"

"Yeah, that's right." Martin confirmed. "And when we've made our first million, I'm going to buy a new set of guitar strings. And a proper plectrum."

"And we've got a manager too and all, and we've practically got a recording deal with a major company already, and we've written a Number One hit single called 'Cadgy Wadgy Woo Woo', so we're almost in the big time already."

"Who's your manager?" Amber demanded.

"My brother Terry," Wilmot said. "He's got a good head for business. He's protecting our talent from ruthless exploitation from crooks."

"Oooh," Amber said. "Your brother Terry. He's nice."

Wilmot pretended he hadn't heard her. He didn't understand it really. How could Amber Watts – who came over as tough as old nails – go all oooey and cooey whenever Terry was around? It made you feel all creepy inside, just like you had a stomach full of spiders. And it wasn't as if Terry gave her any encouragement. He called her names like Marmalade Head and Orange Bonce and Satsuma Face behind her back. It was odd really.

"Well, if you'll excuse us then, we'll get back to our rehearsal," Wilmot said. "Come on, Martin—"

But before Wilmot could even turn his back he heard Amber Watts say six words which chilled his blood and all but turned it to solid ice.

"We want to be in it."

Wilmot played it daft.

"Beg pardon?"

"We want to be in it."

"In what?"

"The band. We want to be pop stars and all, don't we Edith?"

Silent Edith nodded her head.

"But you can't be in our band, can they Martin?"

Martin shook his head.

"Why not?" Amber demanded. "We want to be in it."

"But it's our band."

"Well, when we're in it, it'll be our band as well."

"But we don't want you in it."

"You can't keep us out. You're not allowed to keep girls out of things like that any more. It's all equal opportunities now. If you don't let us in your band it'll be sexism and we'll have the police on you and then you won't be able to have a band at all."

"Yeah but—" Wilmot began, wishing Terry was there to help him out with a few sound reasons as to why Amber and Edith couldn't join the band.

"But nothing. We want to be in your band and be heart-throbs and make millions too and so we're going to be, so there."

"But you can't even play a musical instrument."

"Neither can you two by the sound of it. And anyway, I *can* play an instrument. I can play the violin."

"But you can't have a pop band with a violin in it."

"Yes you can," Amber said. "I've seen it on the telly. One band even had an electric violin. So there."

"Yeah, but what about Edith then," Wilmot floundered, seeming to feel the ground slip away from underneath him. "You can't play anything can you?"

Edith shook her head.

"There you are then," Wilmot said triumphantly. "She can't play so she can't be in it. And you can't leave her out on her own. So you can't be in it either."

"Edith can be in it," Amber said.

"Doing what?" Wilmot demanded.

"Backing vocals." Amber said.

"But she never speaks!" Wilmot all but screamed.

"That's all right," Amber said. "She can do silent backing vocals."

"You can't do silent backing vocals!" Wilmot said, feeling himself in danger of losing his sanity. "Martin, tell her you can't do silent backing vocals."

"That's right," Martin agreed. "You can't. Vocals have to be heard or they're not vocals."

"Edith *can* do silent back vocals. Show them, Edith. Do the silent backing vocals to one of the songs in the top ten."

Edith opened her mouth, tilted back her head, and nothing came out.

"There!" Amber said. "Silent backing vocals, see. I'll get my violin and then we'll climb over the fence and join you in the shed for the band practice."

Wilmot and Martin watched the two girls as they

hurried off towards Amber's house to fetch her violin. There was a vague twanging noise from somewhere nearby, Martin looked down at his guitar, then he nudged Wilmot in the ribs.

"Wilmot," he said, "there's bad news and there's bad news."

"I know," Wilmot told him, "I know."

And he looked across at Martin's guitar to see that there were only three strings left.

The two boys went back into the shed.

6

Starts and Fits

Terry Tanner put his completed homework away in his school bag and opened up the local evening paper. This wasn't because Terry was a great newspaper reader, but he liked to see the daily cartoons, and he liked to look at the television listings in case he needed to try and badger some extra TV time out of his father. He knew that his mum would never let him have any, but his dad was a softer touch and Terry knew how to lean on him and how to apply the necessary pressure.

As he turned the pages of the newspaper, he heard a faint caterwauling coming from the far end of the garden, seemingly from the shed. It was an eerie, almost blood-curdling sound, as if several pairs of fingernails were being dragged down a blackboard all at once. Terry opened the kitchen door and listened attentively, hoping that the sound wasn't what he thought it was. But as he listened he distinctly made out the words, "*Oooeee, Oooeee.*

I'm so free. Feel like a cup of tea. Don't be late. You're my milkshake. Pass me the football. Let me buy you a burger, baby, down at McDonald's. And you can pay for the cokes!" and he realised that it was indeed the sound of Wilmot and Martin practising to be heart-throbs.

"I dunno," Terry thought to himself. "I dunno about this." It wasn't that Wilmot's singing was actually that bad, nor was Martin's three stringed guitar playing. What made the sound so awful was that whatever key Wilmot was singing in, it wasn't the key Martin was playing in, and however slow Wilmot went, Martin was always at least two bars behind him, which meant that when Wilmot came to the chorus, Martin was still playing the verse.

Terry closed the door and went back to the evening paper.

"I dunno," he thought. And it came to him then that Wilmot had failed to take one thing into account in his bid to be pop star and have a Number One in the charts. It was his total lack of talent.

Gloom descended upon Terry as he saw his management fees and earnings vanishing to nothing. What use was half of everything if everything was nothing? He turned another page of the newspaper, the wailing continued out in the garden.

"*Chukky doo wah*!" Wilmot sang loudly, and his voice floated out over the rhododendrons. Terry looked up nervously at the kitchen windows, wondering if he should put some sticky tape over them, just in case they began to crack and glass started flying everywhere.

He turned another page in the newspaper and paused to look at the classified ads to see if there were any top-of-the-range, second hand computers in the Under a Fiver column. It was a slim hope, but there was no harm in looking.

But as he was turning the page over, something else caught his eye. It was a large display ad, in among the cinema listings on the entertainments page.

"Grand Talent Contest," the ad read. "MegaMix Records Inc. presents a Battle of the Bands. Do you have what it takes to be the next George Michael, the next Spice Girls, or the next Oasis? Do you know someone who does? A guaranteed recording contract and record release for the winner. Plus a cash prize of £5,000! Phone or write for application form." And there followed a telephone number and an address.

Terry stared at the ad.

"Grand talent contest," he muttered, glancing out of the window. "Pity it's not a grand *lack* of talent contest. Wilmot would win that hands down. If there was a £5,000 prize for cracking windows without touching them, he'd get top prize, no worries."

But then, just as Terry was thinking this, a most amazing thing happened. Suddenly, from the far end of the garden, came the clear, melodious sound of a violin. It transformed everything and changed what had started off as an awful racket into quite tolerable music. It made even Wilmot's singing sound rather pleasant. It made the whole song sound catchy and tuneful.

"Who," thought Terry, "is that on the fiddle?"

And leaving the newspaper on the kitchen table, he went out into the garden and headed towards the shed.

Terry went to the window first and peeked inside. There was Wilmot, singing for all he was worth, using one of last year's carrots for a microphone. He had obviously devised a few dance steps for himself and had been working on his stage presentation. He wriggled and squirmed as he sang, gyrating his hips first one way, then another.

"Coh," thought Terry, "what's up with Wilmot? He looks like he's desperate for the toilet. Big jobs too by the look of it. Enormous jobs, probably, the way he's twisting about. I don't think he'll be able to hold out much longer. I hope he can last out to the end of the song."

Behind Wilmot, Terry saw Martin, hammering out chords on his three stringed guitar. He seemed to have mislaid his plectrum and was using a potato to strum the guitar.

"I'm not surprised he keeps busting strings," Terry thought, "using a potato. You shouldn't play a guitar with a potato. An apple maybe, or a sprout, but not a potato."

Next he saw Amber, her red hair swept back in a pony tail, her violin under her chin, her bow working skilfully over it, carrying the tune along.

"Amber!" Terry thought. "What's *she* doing in the band? I'll have to boot her out. We don't want her in it, she's a pain in the neck."

But just then Amber played a particularly difficult twiddly bit on the violin.

"On second thoughts," Terry said to himself, "she'd better stay in. She's the only one who's any good. Not that I'll tell her that."

But then Terry saw a sight inside the shed that brought him to the verge of panic. But it was not the time to panic. Panicking was no good. It was action that was needed. At last, it was a real live emergency, a genuine opportunity for heroism, the sort he'd been waiting for for years.

It was Edith. Amber's friend Edith Pearson. She was there in the shed, standing just behind Wilmot, writhing about just like him, as if she desperately needed the toilet too. Only there was more to it than that. In her case her mouth was opening and closing, just like a fish out of water, but no sound at all was coming out.

"Blimey!" thought Terry. "It's Edith Pearson and she's having a fit. That must be it. She's having an epileptic fit, just like they told us about when we did first aid at school. I'd better leap into action and do something to save her life. They don't seem to have noticed what she's doing. She might die at any second."

For a moment, Terry froze. Now, what was the procedure again? His mind raced as he tried to remember. It raced too quickly and went past the information he needed, but then it came back and retrieved it.

"She might swallow her tongue!" Terry thought. "That's it. That's the danger. You can have a fit and fall unconscious and you can swallow your tongue and stop breathing. And what you have to do is get a spoon and put it into the person's mouth to hold their tongue back and stop them choking."

Terry felt in his pocket for spoons. Not a spoon in there.

"Isn't that typical," he thought, "you go around for years with a couple of spoons on you, just in case you happen to meet someone who wants to share a yoghurt or a tub of ice cream with you, and they never do, and come the day you really need a spoon, you haven't got one."

He glanced back into the shed. The song was nearing its end. Wilmot was giving his all, singing into the manky, wrinkled carrot for all he was worth. Bits were flying off the potato as Martin belted his guitar. Amber was moving her violin bow faster than a granny's knitting needle. And Edith—

"Oh, no!" thought Terry. "She's going. She's really having it. She's really having a fit."

And he ran.

* * *

The song was just finishing.

"*Cadgy wadgy choo choo*," Wilmot sang. "*Oh baby if I had to choose between you and my trainers it would be a penalty shootout.*"

The last chords hung in the air. Amber held a note on the violin. Wilmot mopped the sweat from his eyes. And just then—

In burst Terry, kicking the door wide open, so hard it almost fell off its hinges.

"It's Edith!" he yelled. "It's Edith! Quick. She's swallowing her tongue! Get a spoon! Has anyone got a spoon on them?"

"Eh?" Wilmot said. "What are you doing Terry? What's up?"

"What's up? Don't be daft Wilmot. Can't you see it when someone's having a fit!"

"Why, are you having a fit then, Terry? You do seem a bit agitated."

"Not *me*," Terry yelled. "*Her*!" he said, pointing at Silent Edith. "If we don't get a spoon in her mouth she'll die any moment."

"It's the shed, Terry. Not the kitchen. There's no spoons in here. And anyway—"

"All right," Terry said, seizing hold of the garden spade, "we'll have to use the spade then. Wilmot, you and Martin hold her down while I put the spade in her mouth."

Silent Edith started to cry – silently.

"You'll never get the spade in there, Terry," Wilmot reasonably pointed out. "It's too big to go in Edith's mouth."

"We'll have to give it a shove then. It's better than dying."

"Come off it, Terry. Putting spades in people mouths is probably going to kill them anyway."

Terry threw the spade down and grabbed up a trowel instead.

"This'll do," he said. "It's smaller. Get her, Wilmot and we'll save her life."

By now Silent Edith was cowering in a corner of the shed, trembling with fear and very tearful – behaviour which convinced Terry even more that she was on the verge of a fit.

"Come here, Edith," Terry said, as he advanced on her with the trowel. "I'm just going to put this trowel in your gob a minute. But you're not to worry. It's for your own good and your parents will probably thank me and send me a nice card with a book token in it."

Amber stepped in between the trembling Edith

and the approaching Terry. She was as tall as Terry and weighed about the same and she was not a girl to be easily dismissed or shouldered aside.

"You leave my friend alone, Terry Tanner!" she snapped. "I used to fancy you but I don't any more. And if you go near her with that trowel, I'll flatten your head with the watering-can."

"I'd be careful if I were you," Wilmot warned Amber. "Terry's a dangerous man. He knows Boo-Jitsu. He can kill with his bare hands – he says."

"I don't care if he can kill with his bare bottom," Amber sneered.

"He probably can," Wilmot said. "If the smells that come out of it are anything to go by."

"Belt up, Wilmot," Terry snapped. "Or you're a dead man. Come here Edith, I need to do a life saving operation on you."

"So why are you going to kill *me* then and save *her*?" Wilmot asked. "I'm your brother. She's not. Where's your sense of values?"

"Yeah, that's why," Terry said. "If she was my brother I wouldn't bother. If I save her life, there's probably a book token in it. Now move aside Amber," Terry warned, "I'm here to save life. And if I have to kill a few people along the way in order to do that – well, I'm sorry, but it can't be helped."

It looked as if Terry and Amber were bound to come to blows, but then Martin chipped in with a simple, although very pertinent question.

"Why do you think Edith's having a fit, Ter?" he asked.

"I saw her. I looked in through the window and saw her."

The penny dropped.

"Oh, but that wasn't Edith having a fit Terry," Wilmot said. "That was her being in the band."

Terry lowered the trowel. Uncertainty was undermining his resolve.

"In the band?"

"Yeah," Wilmot said.

"Doing what in the band?"

"Backing vocals," Wilmot said.

"But she wasn't singing anything!" Terry yelled.

"Yeah, that's because she's shy, see, and doesn't like talking to people. So she's doing silent backing vocals."

Terry looked around the shed at the four members of the band.

"Silent backing vocals?"

"Yeah," Wilmot nodded. "Silent backing vocals.

You can't hear them, but you can see them."

"You won't be able to see them if you make a record."

"Well dub them in."

For a second Terry was in half a mind to wash his hands of the whole thing. But then his eye for making a pound and his head for business took over. Maybe it wasn't such a bad idea at that. After all, a band needed a gimmick, and it wasn't every group who had a singer who sang into a carrot, a red headed violinist, a guitar player who used a potato instead of a plectrum and a girl doing silent backing vocals.

"All right," Terry said. "Sorry about that little misunderstanding, Edith. No harm intended."

Terry realised that he was still holding the trowel and that Edith was looking at it nervously. He threw it down amongst the other garden tools in a corner.

"Okay, band," Terry said. "I'll let you get on with the rehearsal then and I'll go back to the kitchen and get on with taking care of business. I'll maybe run up a few more contracts or something."

"So what did you come down for then?" Wilmot asked.

"Oh, just to say that I might have a gig for you," Terry said.

"A booking! A booking to play? For the band?"

"Could be. I might have a booking for you very soon, Wilmot, very soon indeed. Any day now, little brother, with my help and guidance and contacts, you could be Number One in the charts."

7

Grooming for Stardom

While the rehearsal continued down in the shed, Terry returned to the kitchen and carefully cut out the advertisement for the Battle of the Bands.

Once he had done so, he went in search of his mother and asked if she had a bottle of any liquid paper or Tipp-ex anywhere.

"What for, Terry?" she said.

"Oh, just a project I'm working on," he mumbled.

His mum looked in her bag but she didn't have any.

"Ask your father," she said. "He might have some somewhere. He's always making mistakes."

Terry found his dad in the living room. He had just turned on the evening news and was shouting at a politician on the screen.

"He doesn't expect us to believe that does he!" he yelled. "Does he think we're *all* stupid? Or just some of us?"

"Have you got any liquid paper, Dad, the white stuff?" Terry asked.

"In my brief case, Terry. Why? What are you doing?"

"Oh, just helping Wilmot, Dad. I'm grooming him for stardom."

"Oh, okay."

When Terry had taken the bottle of Tipp-ex and left the room, Mr Tanner looked wonderingly after him.

"Helping Wilmot?" he thought. "Did he say he was *helping* Wilmot? Terry, *helping* Wilmot?" He wiggled a finger in his ear, in case there was a piece of wax in it.

"I must have misheard," he thought. "That was probably it. I'm imagining things."

At 7.15 that evening Mrs Tanner went down to the bottom of the garden and told Wilmot that it was time to stop the band practice and that Martin ought to be getting home. She was surprised to discover Amber and Edith in the shed as well, for up until then Amber and Wilmot had been sworn enemies.

"I suppose it's making music together that makes the difference," Mrs Tanner thought. "It breaks the barriers down, does music. It's the international language of friendship in many ways. It's good to see them all getting on. Just as long as they don't take it too seriously, all this wanting to be stars."

Later, when the others had gone home and Wilmot was lying in the bath, trying to see whether his heart would stop beating if he held his breath for long enough, Mrs Tanner put her head round the door and said,

"You're not taking this band thing *too* seriously now, are you Wilmot. It is just for fun, isn't it?"

"Oh, don't worry, Mum," Wilmot assured her, "we don't expect to be famous forever. We'll be happy with just a couple of Number Ones and a few million pounds apiece, that'll do us."

"Oh."

"And I'll tell you what, Mum, when I've made my first million, I'll buy you a present, anything you want, Mum. You can have a new ironing board or anything. With gold plated legs, if you like."

"Thank you, Wilmot," Mrs Tanner said, deeply touched. "That's very kind. I've always wanted an ironing board with gold-plated legs. but we'll have to see. Just so long as you don't get your hopes up too high, that's all. I wouldn't want you to be disappointed if it didn't work out as planned."

"No, it's all right, Mum. We'll be okay. Terry's going to be our manager, you see. He's grooming me for stardom."

"Oh, is he now?"

"Yeah, he's doing all the contracts and handling all the money."

"Oh *is* he now?"

"Yeah. He's going to make sure we don't get swindled or ripped off by unscrupulous sharks who exploit young and ambitious children with exceptional musical abilities."

"I see. Yes. Well, if Terry's keeping an eye out for you—" Mrs Tanner began, then she left, muttering the rest of the sentence to herself, "—I'll keep an eye out for Terry."

Wilmot was lying on his bed trying to pen some new song lyrics – aware that one song wouldn't be enough when it came to making the album – when the door opened and Terry walked in.

Wilmot looked up from his writing pad.

"Ever heard of such a thing as knocking?" he asked, irritated at Terry simply walking into his room as if he owned the place.

"Ever heard of such a thing as a wallop on the nose?" Terry said.

Wilmot straighted up.

"Ever heard of such a thing as having a pillow stuffed down your throat?" he asked in turn.

Terry bristled.

"Ever heard of such a thing as having your big toe stuck into the bedside lamp and then having the electricity turned on?" he snapped, his voice growing louder.

"Ever heard of such a thing as getting your hair washed in the toilet bowl and your trousers flushed down the loo?" Wilmot demanded, his voice louder still.

"Ever heard—" Terry began to say, but he was silenced by another voice from somewhere downstairs. It was their mum calling.

"Ever heard of such a thing as pocket money, you two? Because that's another two weeks when you're not getting any. I told you about arguing."

"No, you didn't!" Terry yelled out of the door.

"Yes, she did," Wilmot shouted back. "She told us about not arguing ages ago. She says it every day."

"No, she doesn't!"

"Yes, she does."

"Stop *arguing*!" Mrs Tanner all but screamed.

"I'm not arguing, Mum," Wilmot said, annoyed. "I'm agreeing with you."

"He is not," Terry said. "He's disagreeing with me!"

"I am not!" Wilmot replied.

"BE QUIET AND STOP SHOUTING YOU TWO!" Mrs Tanner yelled.

Their dad came out of the living room then, looked up the stairs, sucked his cheeks in and said, "Aye, aye, aye," in a long suffering voice before going back to the telly.

"What do you want anyway, Terry?" Wilmot asked. "Apart from a lesson in good manners."

But Terry didn't rise to the bait.

"I just came to tell you, Wilmot," he said, "that Terry Tanner Management Limited – the Agent To The Stars – is working on your behalf to put you up there where you belong."

"Up where?" Wilmot said. "In the attic?"

"I mean your name, Wilmot, up in lights. I think, Wilmot, that I may have already found you your first professional engagement and may possibly even have secured you a recording contract. Take a look at this."

He passed Wilmot the Battle of the Bands talent contest advertisement which he had cut from the local evening paper. Wilmot's eyes devoured it greedily. He muttered as he read—"recording contract – guaranteed single release – next big thing—" Then he looked up at Terry.

"Hey, Terry," he said excitedly. Have you seen this? There's a big cash prize. £50, Terry! We could get £50!"

"That's right, Wilmot," Terry said. "It's a lot of money, eh? All you've got to do is win the talent contest, which shouldn't be too much of a problem. Not with the management you've got."

For a fraction of a second a shadow of suspicion seemed to cross Wilmot's face. It was almost like a cloud momentarily blocking out the sun.

"What's the matter, Wilmot?"

"Nothing. It's just this newspaper ad here seems to have a bit of Tipp-ex on it. Like something's been Tipp-exed out."

Terry looked at the newspaper cutting carefully.

"No, Mum or Dad spilt a bit on it I should think, that's all. But just imagine that, eh, Wilmot, fifty quid and a recording contract. That's beyond your wildest imaginings, eh? Just think what you could do with your share of fifty quid."

Another cloud crossed Wilmot's face.

"What do you mean, *my* share? I'd get it *all*, wouldn't I?"

"Well, not entirely, Wilmot, there's management fees and expenses to take care of. Then Martin and Amber and Edith will want a cut – especially Edith, because it's a very specialised job, singing silent back vocals. And then of course you'll have to pay your musician's union subscriptions and your VAT and your milk bills. But I reckon you should clear a tenner easily."

"Oh," Wilmot said, rather crest-fallen.

"What's the matter?"

"I was hoping for more than that. Terry. I've promised Mum a new ironing board, see. I said she could have one with gold-plated legs."

"Sheer extravagance, Wilmot," Terry said. "You'll have to learn to be careful with your money. Not go frittering it away on gold-plated ironing boards. And ten quid's a start, isn't it? So, shall I enter you all for the Battle of the Bands or not? What do you say?"

"Yeah," Wilmot said. "Let's do it. Yeah. Battle of the Bands. Let's go for it, Terry. We're going to be rich and famous and big pop stars. Top of the charts, Terry, you'll see."

"Okay," Terry said, "then in that case I'll ring up for an application form. And we're going to have to think of a name for the band. I thought if I sat in on the drums – well, biscuit tin lids – maybe it could be something like Terry and the Turnip Heads. I could be Terry, you see, and the rest of you could be Turnip Heads."

But Wilmot wasn't keen on this suggestion.

"Just a second," he said. "Whose idea was all this, Ter? Who's the founder member here? Who's the driving force behind all this? Who's the one with all the talent? Me! That's who. Oh no, not Terry and the Turnip Heads. How about something like – Wilmot and the Wallies. I can be Wilmot and the rest of you can be Wallies. You can show the others how to do it, eh, Terry? Because, I mean, you're a sort of total Wally yourself, aren't you? A natural born Wally, some might say."

"Now look, Wilmot," Terry said, getting hold of Wilmot's big toe in a little-known Boo-Jitsu hold. "I've just had about enough of you and your stupid remarks, so I'm going to show you some Boo-Jitsu. Only by the time I've finished with you, it'll be

Boo-Hoo-Jitsu, and you'll be doing the boo-hooing."

"Oh will I now," Wilmot said. And quick as a flash he reached under his pillow and whipped out the brown cardboard inside of an old toilet roll, which he had obviously been hiding there for such emergencies. "In that case, Terry, I'm going to give you a real live demonstration of how the SAS destroy their enemies with the cardboard bit from old toilet rolls. Only by the time you find out how it's done, you'll be too dead to remember anything about it."

But just at that moment Wilmot's bedroom door opened and their mother walked in. Wilmot and Terry looked up together.

"And what do you two think you're doing?!" their mother demanded.

"Hey Mum," Terry and Wilmot said indignantly. "Haven't you heard of knocking."

They lost another year's pocket money for that. And the issue of what to call the band still remained unresolved.

8

Amber and the Assortments

At school the next day, Wilmot told Martin about the forthcoming Battle of the Bands and of the recording contract and the £50 (less management fees and expenses) to be won.

"It's a pity you've only got three strings on your guitar, Martin," Wilmot said. "It would make a big difference to us that, if you had another string or so."

"Well, never mind, Wilmot," Martin said, "you know what they say, three strings are better than one."

Wilmot gave him an odd look.

"No, I don't think that's right, Martin," he said. "It's not three strings, it's two heads."

Martin looked at him blankly.

"It's two heads what?"

"Two heads are better than one."

Martin considered this.

"Not if you've only got one hat," he said.

It was Wilmot's turn to look blank.

"One hat what?"

"If you've only got one hat, then two heads can't be better than one, can they? Because your other head would get wet, wouldn't it? If you didn't have a hat for it. So you shouldn't really say that two heads are better than one, should you? What you should really say is two heads are better than one except when it's raining or unless you've only got one hat."

Wilmot gave Martin a long hard look. He wondered if Martin really was his best friend sometimes or if he wasn't more along the lines of one of those pets you get, which are all right for about a fortnight, but then they turn into annoying nuisances that keep going to the toilet on the carpet when you're not looking.

"I think I'm getting a headache," Wilmot told him.

"Good job you've only got one head then," Martin said. " 'Cause otherwise you'd have two headaches. In which case, two heads would be worse than one, wouldn't they, eh, Wilmot?"

Wilmot had the distinct feeling that he wasn't really getting anywhere with Martin. But fortunately the whistle blew and they had to go into class.

"Band rehearsal. My shed. Tonight," Wilmot whispered as they filed into assembly. "Very important meeting. We're going to have to think of a name for the band, okay?"

Martin nodded.

"Should be okay," he said. "I'll bring my axe."

"Bring your guitar as well," Wilmot said, wondering why Martin would want to chop anything up. Maybe he needed some firewood at home.

"No," Martin whispered, "that's what these big rock stars call their guitars – *axes*. They say, 'Play that axe, man', and stuff like that."

"Right," said Wilmot, wanting to be in with the hip sayings, "Cool. Gimme four, man."

"You mean five don't you?" Martin said.

"No," Wilmot said. "I've got a splinter in my little finger and I don't want it bashed."

Just then the voice of their teacher, Mr Phelps, boomed across the hall.

"Wilmot Tanner, are you talking?"

"No, Mr Phelps," Wilmot said. "I was whispering."

"Then do it quietly," Mr Phelps commanded.

Wilmot stared at Martin. Do it quietly? How else could you do whispering? The world was going mad.

"I'll be glad when I'm a heart-throb," Wilmot thought, "with loads of money and a house in the country with a private swimming pool. I'll have my own private school too. I won't have to come here at all then. I'll have a private sweet shop as well. And a private dentist. And my own private roller-coaster. And my own private dungeon for Terry. Roll on being rich and famous. I can hardly wait."

Rehearsals began promptly at six o'clock that night, straight after tea, down in Wilmot's shed. Although not invited to attend (as the actual membership of the still unnamed band remained on an informal basis) Amber Watts and her friend Silent Edith Pearson heard the pulsating rhythms of three stringed guitar and comb and tissue paper echoing in the cool evening air. Amber ran to fetch her violin and she and Edith climbed over the fence.

Each – unknown to the other – had been practising in front of the mirror at home. Edith had worked out a complicated dance routine to perform while she did the silent backing vocals. The routine ended with her doing a handstand, followed by a back-flip, followed by the splits – though the last part was more by way of an accident than design.

Although her contribution to the sound of the band was nil, Edith added a huge visual element to it which was bound to go down well with the Battle of the Bands judges.

The first time she tried her back-flip in the narrow confines of Wilmot's shed, she upset a stack of plastic flowerpots and landed head first in a bag of manure. Wilmot then suggested that she should change her name from Silent Edith to Incredibly Stinky Edith or even to Compost Face. But once Edith had shown him a few of the things she had learned at Self Defence For Girls down at the leisure centre – where she did Women's-Lib-Jitsu every Friday – Wilmot stopped making cracks at her expense and concentrated more on the music.

"A one, a two, a one two three – what comes next again? Oh yeah, four, that's it! take it away!" he said, and he blew for all he was worth into his comb and tissue paper.

The sounds of "Cadgy Wadgy Woo Woo" once more rent the quiet of the evening. Mrs Tanner closed the kitchen window as the cat ran off into the sitting room and hid up the chimney.

"What *is* Wilmot doing?" she said. "He seems to

be taking this band thing very seriously. Anyone would think there was money in it or something." She looked across at Terry who was sitting at the kitchen table making some kind of list on a piece of paper which was headed Plan of Campaign and Management Strategy (Terry Tanner Management and Production Ltd. Agent To The Stars.)

Under the main heading was a reminder list of things to do. Some were obvious, others were more obscure. "Band Name," the list said; "Agency Fees," it went on, then "Leather trousers?" it read followed by the words, "More gimmicks?" followed by a note reading "Get Wilmot to shave his head?" and "Get Wilmot to have his nose pierced?" and finally "Get Wilmot to have a tattoo? I could do this on the cheap for him with a biro."

"Do you know what they're up to down there, Terry?" Mrs Tanner asked.

"Sorry, Mum?"

"Wilmot and the others, down in the shed?"

"Rehearsing Mum, we're maybe going in for a talent contest."

Mrs Tanner looked at Terry doubtfully.

"Talent?" she said. "Wilmot?"

Terry didn't reply.

"You're not trying to take advantage of Wilmot at all, are you Terry?"

Terry looked up at her. His face a picture of hurt emotions.

"Me, Mum?" he said. "Take advantage of little Wilmot, my very own brother? Would I do a thing like that? No, I'm just trying to help him realise his ambitions, Mum, and protect him from greedy and unscrupulous people."

"Oh, all right then," Mrs Tanner said. She looked towards the end of the garden. The shed had fallen quiet. "Talent contest, eh?"

"Nothing serious, Mum," Terry said. "Just a bit of fun really. I shouldn't think anyone in the band will make any money out of it."

"Yes. It seems to have gone very quiet down there now. I wonder what they're up to."

The cat came back into the kitchen, trailing a path of dark, black soot behind him. Mr Tanner followed him.

"Look at me!" he said. "Look at my shirt! I was sitting reading the paper when the cat came down the chimney and tried to hide up my pullover."

"Well, I say we should call the band Amber and the

Assortments," Amber said. "I can be Amber and you can be the Assortments."

"Do you now," Martin said. "Well, *I* say we should call it Martin and Wilmot and the Morons. I can be Martin and Wilmot can be Wilmot and you two girls can be—"

Silent Edith grasped the sleeve of Amber's sweat-shirt and tugged at it to get her attention.

"Hang on," Amber said, "Edith wants to say something."

She leant down and put her ear close to Edith's mouth while Edith whispered something to her.

"Okay," Amber nodded. "I'll tell them."

She straightened up.

"Well?" Martin asked. "What'd she say?"

"She suggested that we could call the band Silent Edith and Amazing Amber and the Screwballs. She says she can be Edith and I can be Amber and you two can be a couple of—"

"No way," Wilmot said. "No way am I being billed as one half of the Screwballs. Whose band is this anyway, after all? Whose idea was it? Who's the creative force behind it all? Me, that's who. So I say we call it the Wilmots and have done with it."

"Maybe," Martin said – tactfully trying to diffuse

the atmosphere – "it might be better if we didn't have anyone's name in the band title. Then there wouldn't be any arguing."

"Good idea," Amber said. "Let's call the band The Pepper Girls."

"*Girls*?" Wilmot said. "Martin and me aren't *girls*!"

"I can lend you a skirt," Amber said.

"Get lost," Wilmot told her. "We're not having girls in the title."

"Unless we called the band Boys and Girls," Martin suggested.

"Girls and Boys," Amber said.

"Or Boys Meet Girls?" Wilmot suggested.

"Girls Meet Boys," Amber said.

"Or how about Boys Meet Girls And Give Girls A Good Punch In The Head?" Wilmot asked, feeling that this discussion had gone on long enough.

Edith tugged at Amber's sleeve and whispered into her ear again.

"What's she say now?"

"She says how about Girls Give Boys A Good Kicking In Their Dirty Bits?"

"No," Martin said, "that's too long."

"Boyz 'N Girlz then," Wilmot said. "With zeds. It's my band and that's my best offer."

The four of them looked at each other. After a few seconds Amber nodded.

"Okay," she said, "Boyz 'N Girlz, with zeds. What do you say, Edith?"

Edith nodded.

"Right," Martin said, relieved that the bickering was over, "Boyz 'N Girlz it is. With zeds. Now let's get on with the rehearsal."

They had another run through of "Cadgy Wadgy Woo Woo". During the song there was a persistent knock knock, knocking coming from somewhere nearby.

"What was that?" Martin asked. "Was it a wood-pecker?"

Wilmot took a quick look outside.

"No," he said, "it was just Mr Ronson next door, he's out in the garden hitting himself over the head with a plank of wood."

"Why's he doing that?" Martin asked.

"I don't know," Wilmot said. "People do funny things when they get older. Maybe he's having a turn."

They packed in the rehearsal round about seven.

Just as Amber was putting her violin back in its case, and just as Wilmot was putting his comb back into his pocket and blowing his nose on his tissue paper, the shed door opened and Terry entered carrying four pieces of paper.

"Okay, band," he said. "Good practice. I could hear you in the kitchen. You're really improving. The cat's stopped hiding up the chimney. So either you're getting better or he's getting used to it. Now, have you thought of a name yet?"

"Boyz 'N Girlz," Wilmot told him. "With zeds."

"Yeah," Terry said. "I like that. It's good. With zeds. Nice touch."

"I thought of it," Wilmot said proudly.

"Did you?" Terry said. "Still, never mind. Okay then," he said. "Now if you can just all sign these contracts here, appointing me as official manager—"

He handed out pens and sheets of paper. Three of the contracts had writing on them and could only be described as fair and reasonable. But Wilmot stared at the paper he was given. It seemed different from the other three.

"What's this?" he said.

"It's your contract," Terry told him.

"But I've already signed a contract. Two of them!"

"This is a new contract. You can never have too many contracts, Wilmot."

"But there's nothing written here," Wilmot said. "It's blank."

"Yeah," said Terry. "I'll fill in the details later. I didn't have time to write yours out."

"Well, I hope I can trust you," Wilmot said, hesitating a moment before accepting the pen.

"Trust me?" Terry said. "Wilmot, I'm your brother, aren't I?!"

"Yeah," Wilmot muttered. "That's what I mean."

9

Big Fat Bits

The next morning the post arrived just as Terry and Wilmot were about to leave for school. A large white envelope franked with the words MegaMix Records Inc. Battle of the Bands fell through the letterbox, addressed to one Mr. T. Tanner Esquire (Agent To The Stars).

"Terry," Mr Tanner said, just about to leave for work, "one for you here. It says something about 'stars' too. What's that supposed to mean?"

"Probably my astronomy catalogue," Terry said. "I sent off for a telescope brochure."

"Any for me, Dad?" Wilmot asked hopefully.

"No, Wilmot, afraid not."

"I don't think that postmen likes me," Wilmot said. "He never brings me any letters. I think there's some kind of conspiracy going on down at the sorting office."

"I don't think it's quite that, Wilmot," his father said. "I think if you want to get letters sent to you,

you first have to write to people yourself."

"I do," Wilmot said. "I wrote to my pen pal in the Philippines, but he still hasn't written back."

"You should never have sent him your photograph, Wilmot," Terry said. "He probably opened that envelope, took one look at you and fell into a coma."

"Watch it, Terry," Wilmot said, "or you'll accidentally fall into the dustbin, head first."

"Now, now," Mr Tanner said. "That's enough. Hurry up and get ready." And he went off in search of his bicycle clips.

Terry tore open his envelope.

"Hey, it's the entry form, Wilmot," he said, "for the Battle of the Bands. All the terms and conditions and what you stand to win and all about the prize money and all the rest."

"Well, let's have a look at it then," Wilmot said, reaching for the letter. "Let's see what it says."

But Terry snatched the letter out of his grasp and hurried off with it. "I'll let you look at it in a minute, Wilmot, I've just – just – just need to blow my nose."

Terry hurried up to the spare bedroom – which served as their dad's study and where he did the household accounts – and he rummaged through the drawers there until he found what he wanted – another bottle of liquid paper.

A few seconds later he came back down the stairs, waving the letter and blowing on it.

Wilmot looked at him in puzzlement.

"What're you blowing on the letter for? It's not hot, is it?"

"Me? Blowing? No, I'm just – just whistling, Wilmot, that's all. Just doing – silent whistling that's all. Come on, I'll walk with you to school."

They called out their goodbyes and set off down the road, bags in hand, homework and lunch boxes packed.

"Come on then, Terry, let's have a look at the letter," Wilmot said.

But Terry waved the letter about in the breeze.

"In a second Wilmot, no hurry."

"What are you waving it about for, like you were trying to get it to dry or something?"

"Me? No. I'm not waving it about. Wilmot, I'm just doing my wrist exercises. It's all part of Boo-Jitsu, you see. All in the wrist."

"Come on!"

Finally Terry let Wilmot see the letter.

"Cor," he said. "The Battle of the Bands is in three weeks' time, that's not long."

"No," Terry agreed. "Not long to wait."

"And it tells you all about the recording contract here too."

"That's right."

"And the prize money."

"That's it."

"The £50."

"A lot of money eh, Wilmot. A king's ransom that is to a boy of your age."

Wilmot stopped in his tracks and stared hard at the letter.

"There's Tipp-ex on this," he said.

"Is there?" Terry asked, surprised. "Where?"

"Here!" Wilmot said. "Right here. Just next to this bit about the £50 prize money."

"Must have been the secretary who sent out the letters. Must have spilt a drop," Terry said, hurriedly taking the letter back.

"Oh," Wilmot said uncertainly. "Are you sure?"

But Terry quickly changed the subject.

"Ah, now look here, Wilmot, it says that when you return the application form, you have to send in a demo tape of your band."

"Demo?"

"Demonstration."

"Oh."

"Yeah, it's probably to eliminate the no-hopers."

"Oh," Wilmot said. "We've got to send a tape in, have we? Oh."

He seemed a bit downcast.

"Yes," Terry said. He seemed rather deflated too.

"It's a pity you have to send off a tape in some ways," Wilmot said, "because I feel that really we're more of a live band. You have to see us, to appreciate us fully. We're more something to look at than to listen to. I mean, you have to see it to believe it, really."

"Yeah," Martin agreed. "You probably do."

"Especially with Edith and her silent backing vocals. You do have to see that kind of thing. It doesn't come over so well on record. I mean, if you could see and hear us, like on Top of The Pops, we'd be number one, no worries. But we are a very visual band."

"Yeah, well, let *me* worry about that, Wilmot," Terry said. "I'm your manager after all. I'm here to take all the worries off your shoulders and all the money out of your pockets – that is look after your money for you. I'll deal with the business side and leave you free to be creative. Because you're good at creating, aren't you Wilmot."

"Yes, I suppose so," Wilmot agreed. "In fact I was wondering if I shouldn't get some leather trousers, me being so creative and all."

"Yes, Terry said," I was thinking that. "And I thought maybe you could get your nose pierced. A lot of pop stars have that."

Wilmot stopped at the corner.

"Nose pierced?" he said. "How would I do that?"

"I could do it for you now," Terry offered. "Hang on. I'll just get my hole-punch out of my bag."

"No way," Wilmot said. "I'm not having you use your hole punch on my nose. I'm not going to end up in a ring binder."

"Well, how about if I just punched your nose, then? How would that suit you?"

"Watch it, Terry, I'm warning you."

"Well how about a tattoo then, Wilmot? Because you have to be a bit trendy and cool, you know, to be a pop star."

Wilmot considered this suggestion. He shook his head.

"I don't think Mum would like that, Terry, me

having a tattoo. I mean, it wouldn't wash off, would it?"

"It needn't be a big one," Terry said. "Just a little dragon on your forehead, or a skull and crossbones on your arm. Or you could have a dotted line tattooed round your neck with In Case Of Emergency Cut Here written on it. I've seen people with that. Or you could maybe get your eight times table tattooed on your arm, or get Feed Me, I'm Hungry tattooed onto your lip. Or get Big Disgusting Fat Bits tattooed on to your stomach. Or Mr Stinky tattooed on your bum."

"Yeah," Wilmot said, "and you could get Please Wash Me tattooed under your armpits, Terry. And Please Get This Out Of My Nose tattooed onto your finger!"

"Look, I'm only trying to help you, Wilmot. There's no need to be rude."

"No, well, I don't think so, Terry. I don't think a tattoo would be a good idea. If I got a tattoo and Mum saw it, there'd be no pocket money ever again for the rest of all eternity."

"Yeah," Terry agreed. "Maybe you're right, Wilmot. Not such a good idea the tattoo. No. Mum would go bananas. Well, look, how about shaving your head then?"

Wilmot looked at him.

"Shave it?"

"Yeah. Your head. A lot of pop stars do that – shave their heads. And you can shave off your eyebrows as well. Or maybe you could grow a moustache."

"What?" Wilmot said. "On my head?"

"No, on your lip!"

"I'm not old enough," Wilmot said, "to grow moustaches. It was bad enough growing that mustard and cress."

"Well, you think about it anyway, Wilmot," Terry said. "As your manager I'm advising you that you ought to have a gimmick. Meantime, if you can get the band together tonight, I'll get hold of a tape recorder so we can do the demo."

They were at the gates of the school by now, where Terry went his older way, and Wilmot went his younger one.

"I hope our tape gets chosen," Wilmot said. "Or we won't even *be* in the Battle of the Bands. And then I'll *never* be a pop star."

"You let me worry about all that, Wilmot," Terry

said. "You leave that to your manager."

The two brothers went their separate ways then, and joined their own friends.

But for some reason, Wilmot couldn't stop thinking about the letter – the letter from the recording company. There was something odd about it. Something very odd. It was that blob of Tipp-ex, the liquid paper. There had been a blob of Tipp-ex on the newspaper ad which Terry had shown him too. And almost in the same place, right next to the announcement of the prize money.

Strange that. Very strange. Wilmot had a peculiar feeling about that. All those blobs of liquid paper. He had a very strange feeling about that indeed.

But he didn't quite know why.

10

A Dose of Salts

For the third night running the sound of "Cadgy Wadgy Woo Woo" was coming out from the shed at the far end of Wilmot Tanner's garden. The Tanners' neighbours – Mr and Mrs Ronson – were up in their back bedroom packing a suitcase.

"It can't go on much longer," Mr Ronson said to his wife. "It's probably just a fad. Did you remember to cancel the milk?"

"Yes," she nodded. "And the newspapers. I think a short holiday will do us both a world of good. I must remember to pack my earplugs too."

"I've already got mine in," Mr Ronson said, "for all the good they're doing." And he looked balefully out of the window towards next door's garden shed. "Do you think they know any other songs?"

"Maybe they'll have learned some," Mrs Ronson said, "by the time we get back."

But she didn't sound too hopeful.

* * *

Terry Tanner played back the cassette recording but the quality was not good.

"Okay," he said. "We'll go again. The balance is out. Wilmot, not so loud on the comb and tissue paper solo this time. And Edith, could you bring up those silent backing vocals a little as they're not coming over."

"The violin sounded good though, didn't it?" Amber Watts said, preening, as if she knew her own worth. "I'm learning the violin by the Suzuki method, you know."

"What, on a motorbike?" Wilmot asked.

"Don't be stupid, Wilmot Tanner," Amber said. "It's a way of learning music. It's nothing to do with motorbikes. That's a different Suzuki altogether."

"The guitar was okay and all wasn't it?" Martin said, hoping for a small compliment or two.

"The three *missing* strings sounded good," Amber said. "I'm not sure about the others though, the ones that are still there. Maybe if you broke those as well it might sound a whole lot better."

"Come on," Terry commanded, rewinding the tape. "No squabbling. Let's go for another take, and make it a good one this time. Okay, Wilmot, when you're ready."

"Okay," Wilmot said. "I'll count us in. A one, a two, a one, two, three – what comes after that again? I keep forgetting."

"Stop messing around, Wilmot," Terry said. "You're wasting time. And this is all coming out of your prize money you know."

Wilmot put down his comb.

"What's coming out of my prize money *now*? Or rather, what *else* is coming out of my prize money?"

"My fees," Terry said. "As record producer."

Wilmot looked at his brother in disgust.

"You'll want money for breathing next, you will, Terry, you're that grasping."

"I've already charged for that," Terry told him. "So come on. Take number eight, recording *now*!"

The sound of "Cadgy Wadgy Woo Woo" came out of the shed again. It was the last thing Mr Ronson heard as he backed his car out of the garage and set off in the direction of Bournemouth.

Later that night, when Martin, Amber and Silent Edith had gone home, Wilmot and Terry Tanner sat in the living room replaying the tape of the evening's recording session.

"Sounds pretty good to me," Wilmot said. "I never

knew I was such a good singer. I'm practically a boy soprano."

"You're practically a boy foghorn, more like," Terry said. "You're out of tune."

"It wasn't me," Wilmot said. "It was the others."

Terry hit the fast forward button and sped the tape on to the next take.

"This one's a bit better," he said.

"Yeah," Wilmot agreed. "Just listen to that comb and tissue paper. Talent in the raw that is. That's the one to send off if you ask me, Ter."

"Yeah, maybe," Terry said, non-committally. "Well, you leave it with me, Wilmot. I'll just copy it over to another tape and I'll take care of the application form and all that."

"Okay, Terry."

"You go and have a good soak in the bath then, Wilmot. You deserve to relax after giving it your all in the recording session like that. I know it can't be easy for you creative types."

"You sure you don't mind doing the boring paperwork, Terry?"

"Not at all."

"You think the tape's really good enough for us to be chosen for the Battle of the Bands?"

"Em – I think we'll be able to sort out something, Wilmot."

"I'd be very disappointed if we weren't chosen."

"Me too."

"Especially when there's £50 at stake."

"Yeah quite. Anyway, you go and have a soak in the bath, Wilmot. You can use Mum's best bath salts if you like."

"Oh, can I Terry? Thanks."

"No trouble, little brother. You deserve it."

So Wilmot went off upstairs to have a long soak in his mum's best bath salts while Terry remained in the living room, planning his next move.

"There is no way," Terry thought, "that we're going to be chosen for the Battle of the Bands on the strength of that recording. We're going to need a different approach. Now let me see."

He sat and thought a moment. As he did, his eyes glanced round the room. There, next to the stereo, he saw his dad's old record collection. Among the CDs there were old long-playing records from way back, records of all the old bands, the Rolling Stones, Led Zeppelin, Bob Dylan (and *he* certainly couldn't sing) and of course The Beatles.

And that was when Terry got his next BIG IDEA.

He went upstairs to the spare bedroom where his dad was busy with the gas bill, trying to work out whether the gas company had swindled him or not.

"Dad," Terry said.

"Yes, Terry? I'm rather busy right now."

"Do you mind if I tape some of your old records?"

Mr Tanner looked up from the calculator. An expression of pleasure and delight crossed his face.

"Tape my records? The old ones? No, I don't mind, Terry. That'll be fine. You help yourself. No, glad for you to listen to them. Hear some real music. None of this techo stuff and what have you. No, you help yourself. You listen to some real tunes."

"Okay, Dad, thanks," Terry said, and he went back downstairs.

His father watched him go. He felt pleased, satisfied, justified even.

"He's growing up is Terry," he thought. "He's maturing in his musical tastes. He can see the value of the older stuff. I'm glad about that. Very glad indeed."

Half an hour later, Terry had his tape ready to send off. He put a sticker on the cassette and another on the box and marked them both "Boyz N Girlz (with zeds). Demo Tape. Manager Mr T. Tanner Esquire. Agent To The Stars." He then put the tape into a Jiffy bag together with the application form, went and borrowed some stamps from his mother, and got permission to run down to the post box and catch the last collection.

When he returned it was to find Wilmot and his mother having a stand-up row in the bathroom. Or rather a stand-up, lie-down row, because although Mrs Tanner was standing up, Wilmot was lying down in the bath, up to his ears in bubbles. In fact the bubbles had actually slipped over the side of the bath and were even now creeping towards the rim of the toilet bowl and onwards, out to the landing.

"My expensive bath salts!" Terry heard his mother saying, as he came into the hall. "You used *all* of my expensive bath salts, Wilmot! *All* of them! Why?! Whatever put it into your head! Whoever said you could do a thing like that! Whoever gave you permission to use my best bath salts!"

"Terry did," Wilmot answered. "He said you wouldn't mind."

Terry tiptoed up the stairs, hoping to make it to his bedroom undetected. Unfortunately a floorboard creaked just as he got to the top.

"Terry Tanner!" his mother's voice called from the bathroom. "Is that you? Well, come here!"

Reluctantly, Terry headed for the bathroom.

He had a feeling that pocket money was about to be cancelled for another ten years at the least.

11

Garden Shed Road

There were no rehearsals for the next seven days down at the Tanner "Garden Shed Road" Recording Studios, as everyone was busy with homework, sports practices, Beavers, Brownies and various family commitments.

It was Wilmot who had given the place the name Garden Shed Road. His dad had been going on once again about his beloved Beatles and how he himself could almost have been a pop star and a world famous song writer – if it hadn't been for his bad back and him losing his bicycle clips at the crucial moment and so missing his chance for stardom.

"And The Beatles' best records, Wilmot," he said, "were recorded in London at the Abbey Road studios. And they're now famous the whole wide world over. And people come from as far as Alaska, just to walk down Abbey Road and to say that they've been there."

Somehow, this stuck in Wilmot's mind, and he

brooded over it during the next few days. He could see in his mind's eye all the years ahead. He could see his many fans coming on pilgrimages from as far afield as Alaska, searching for the roots of Boyz 'N Girlz (with zeds) and for the origins of their star songwriter, singer and lead comb and tissue paper player, Wilmot (Dreamboat) Tanner and their lead guitarist Martin (The Mad Axeman) Coombs.

"I think," Wilmot said to Martin, "that we should call our rehearsal rooms Shed Road. Yeah, Garden Shed Road, I think that's what we should call it. It'll be like Abbey Road, and The Beatles. What do you reckon, Martin?"

"Yeah," Martin agreed. "Good thinking, Wilmot. People will come and see your garden shed, and they'll think, 'Cor, so this is Garden Shed Road, this is where a legend was born.' "

"That's right," Wilmot agreed. "They'll look at it and think, 'This is the place where Wilmot Tanner composed his first big hit, right here where his dad used to hang his onions up and pot his seedlings."

"Yeah," Martin said, "they'll think, 'This is the very shed where Martin The Mad Axeman Coombs invented three string guitar playing with half an old potato for a plectrum.' "

"Yeah," Wilmot said, "It'll be like a shrine. It'll be a holy place in years to come, Martin. Garden Shed Road. It'll go down in history."

Just the same, Wilmot was glad to have a few days off. It was all well and good, getting ready to be a heart-throb and being groomed for stardom, but you liked to sit down in front of the telly and watch the odd episode of Star Trek too, just like ordinary people.

And Wilmot was determined to remain ordinary, at whatever costs.

"I won't let fame and fortune change me, Terry," he told his brother one night when they were reluctantly having a bath together due to their mother's insistence on economies.

"No, I shouldn't think fame and fortune will change you, Wilmot," Terry agreed. "You'll probably still be a stupid idiot no matter what you do."

"I mean," Wilmot said, irritated, "that I won't get big headed – like some I could name who're big headed already. I mean I'll still do ordinary things like go shopping at the supermarket."

"But you don't go shopping at the supermarket," Terry pointed out.

"I push the trolley round for Mum," Wilmot said, "that's almost shopping."

"No it isn't! That's just pushing. That's not proper shopping."

"It is too!" Wilmot said. "And what's that you're doing in the bath, Terry?" he demanded. "What are those bubbles? Are you being disgusting again!?"

"If anyone's disgusting," Terry said, "it's you Wilmot. So watch it or I'll bang your head against the taps."

"You watch it yourself, Terry," Wilmot said, "or I'll ram this sponge so far up your nostril it'll be coming out of your ear! And then I'll stick this piece of soap up your other nostril. And then I'm going to take the bath plug and shove it right up—"

"Okay, Wilmot, you asked for this!" Terry said, and he reached out for a large yellow plastic duck which he had had since he was a baby. "I'm going to do a Mr Quackers on you!"

"Okay, Terry! Just you try it," Wilmot said, reaching for his toy submarine, which he had had since he was small. "Because I'm going to torpedo your big fat belly button!"

It was their mother who was the first to notice the

water coming through the living room ceiling. There wasn't a lot of it – at least not to start with – just the odd drop or two plip-plopping on to the chandelier.

"What's that noise, John?" she asked.

"Don't know," Mr Tanner said. "It's odd isn't it. Sounds like rain."

Then he looked up and saw the water running down the light fittings. Mrs Tanner's gaze followed his. Neither of them spoke immediately. They simply watched in horror as the water went on trickling into the chandelier bowl.

Then Mrs Tanner stood up.

"I think I might go up," she said calmly, "and have a quiet word with Wilmot and Terry. I suspect they may be fighting in the bath again, and knocking all the water over the sides."

"I'll go if you like," Mr Tanner offered.

"No, that's okay, thanks," she said. "I think I can manage. You carry on watching the news, dear." And she left the room.

A few moments later, pocket money was cancelled for another fifteen years.

12

A Funny Sort of Letter

On Saturday morning, another letter arrived addressed to Terry Tanner Management Incorporated (Agent To The Stars) again franked MegaMix Records Inc., Battle of the Bands.

It was Wilmot who found the letter lying on the doormat, and he hurried up with it to Terry's room.

"Terry!" he yelled. "It's come! It must be about the Battle of the Bands. About whether we were successful or not. Open it, come on, quick! Let's see if they liked our demo tape of Cadgy Wadgy Woo Woo or not."

Unfortunately Terry was still asleep when Wilmot said all this, so he had to wake him up and say it all over again.

Curiously, Terry showed a marked reluctance to open the letter in front of Wilmot and insisted that he be left alone to read it.

"But I want to know, Terry, if we're in the Battle of the Bands or not. If we've got a chance of getting the recording contract and winning the £50."

"I appreciate that, Wilmot," Terry said, "but this is a solemn and a sacred moment for me. As your appointed agent and representative, it is for me to open the envelope. If the news is good, Wilmot, you will be the first to know. If the news is bad, I will bear the pain alone, and I shall try my best to shield and protect you from disappointment and grief. You can rely on me, Wilmot. I have your best interests at heart. Go now and leave me to brave this moment alone. I shall open this envelope in loneliness and solitude, just as I lie here in my pyjamas with the dried cornflakes down the front from yesterday's breakfast. And if I have failed you, Wilmot, in my efforts to get to the top – well – I shall know what to do, Wilmot, in my sorrow and shame. So close the door behind you, Wilmot, and give me a few moments alone. Farewell, Wilmot – at least for now – or maybe it might be – goodbye."

Wilmot stared at Terry. He felt deeply moved by Terry's words. Sometimes he suspected that Terry was always trying to get one over on him. But on this occasion, there could be no doubting his sincerity.

"Okay, Terry," he said. "I'll be waiting, just outside on the landing. And if it's bad news, Terry –

and I never see you again – well, it was nice knowing you, Ter, even if you do leave big tide marks in the bath."

"It was nice knowing you too, Wilmot," Terry said. "Even if your socks do smell and your underwear's a disgrace."

Then Wilmot left the room and softly closed the door behind him.

The instant he was gone, Terry leapt out of bed, tore open the letter, and quickly read what it had to say:

> *Dear Mr Tanner,* the letter read, *Thank you for sending on the demo tape of the band Boyz 'N Girlz (with zeds) which you are managing. We think you have assembled a very talented collection of individuals here, if the demo tape is anything to go by. The band's versions of those classic songs by the Beatles and the Rolling Stones are truly amazing. They are so close to the original recordings, they could almost have been the real thing. Such a multi-talented, chameleon-like bunch of musicians, able to imitate any band they choose, are a genuine rarity. We have great pleasure therefore in inviting Boyz 'N Girlz (with zeds) to take part in our Battle of*

the Bands at the Winter Gardens Pavilion. Perhaps the band also has some original material which they might care to perform on this occasion.

Thank you again for such a high standard of entry. Full details of the Battle of the Bands contest and the £5,000 cash prize are enclosed. We look forward to seeing you on the day.

Yours sincerely,

Hiram B. Fireum. Managing Director.

MegaMix Records Inc.

P.S. I would be grateful if you could forward a photograph of the band for publicity purposes.

Terry grinned to himself.

"Done it," he said. "We're on the way."

But his elation was short lived. There was a soft tap on his bedroom door and Wilmot's voice called plaintively from the landing.

"Terry? Are you all right? Is it good news, Terry, or have you ended it all? It's just, if you have ended it all, I maybe ought to tell Mum, as she's doing eggs for breakfast and it would be a waste if she did you one and you weren't alive to eat it. Though I could always have it for you, I suppose."

"No, it's all right, Wilmot," Terry called back. "It's

good news. We're in! We're in the Battle of the Bands!"

"Are we? Are we? I'm really going to be a pop star. Am I, Ter? Quick, let's see the letter!" He rattled the door knob. "Here, Terry – why's your door locked?"

"Em – I'll be down to show you the letter in a sec, Wilmot. I suddenly remembered something I've got to do. I've just got to finish up an essay for school – just got to print it out – Dad let me do it on his word processor. Won't be a tick. Just got to go to the study."

So Wilmot went downstairs and Terry hurried to the study in the spare bedroom. He fired up the word processor and did some frantic typing. A few minutes later he ambled into the kitchen.

"Can I see that letter now?" Wilmot asked.

"What letter?" Terry asked, looking blank.

"The one from the record company."

"Oh, that one!"

Terry casually handed Wilmot the envelope. He extracted a piece of paper.

"It's not on headed notepaper this time," Wilmot said, surprised.

"They ran out," Terry said. "Read it for yourself."

So Wilmot smoothed out the letter and he read as follows.

Dear Mr Tinner,
Thank you for sending us the monster tape of the band Boyz 'N Girlz (with nits) that you are managing. We think you have assembled a dead talented load of musikians here. They are truly amazing and so we have grate pleasure in inviting Boyz 'N Girlz (with zits) to take part in our Bottle of the Bends at the Winter Gardens Pavillion.
Full detales of the contest and the huge **£50** *cash prize are enclosed. We look forward to seeing you on the day.*
Yours sincerely,
Hiram B. Fireum. Managing Director.
MegaMix Records Inc.
Pee S.I would be greatful if you could forward a photogruph of the bund for publicity porpoises.
Pee Pee S. Excuse the poor typeing. My seceretarry is off with a coff and I am doing this myself with one finger and without my glasses, and I have also run out of headed notepaper.

Wilmot put the letter down. Then he picked it up and re-read it.

"It's a funny sort of letter this, Terry, isn't it?"

"How do you mean?" Terry said casually. "In what way?"

"Well, this typing and all this mis-spelling. It doesn't look right to me. I mean, you'd expect a managing director to type a bit better than this. This is so bad it almost makes *your* spelling look good."

"My spelling's better than yours Wilmot," Terry bristled. "At least I don't spell elephant with an *f*."

"No. You spell arm-pit with an '*n*' though, don't you?" Wilmot snapped. "And you're always putting a '*p*' in swimming baths."

"Belt up," Terry glared. "Anyway, maybe this bloke is a bit dyslexic. He's probably used to just dictating stuff and not typing it himself, that's all."

Wilmot felt uneasy with this explanation, and yet he couldn't quite think why. Maybe he was being unduly suspicious again. He also wanted to ask Terry who Dick Lexic was – perhaps he'd been a famous highwayman in olden days, like Dick Turpin – but he decided to leave it, as he didn't want to seem ignorant and have Terry sneer at him.

"Yeah, well, never mind," he said. "The point is, we're in, eh, Terry! We're going to be in the Battle of the Bands. So they must have really liked our demo tape, eh?"

"Oh yes," Terry nodded. "It certainly seems that way."

"We're going to win that £50 Terry!"

"We sure are, Wilmot," Terry said. "And it's a lot of money is £50."

"Wait till I tell Martin," Wilmot grinned. "Oh, and I see they want a photo of us. We'd better get that done and all. Maybe this weekend, eh? Maybe Dad'll let us borrow his Polaroid camera."

"Yeah, I should think so," Terry said, rather uncertainly. "He might."

"I'll get on the phone to Martin then," Wilmot said. "And I suppose I'd better tell Amber as well. Photo call this Saturday then, eh? In the shed? After lunch?"

"Yeah, okay then, Wilmot," Terry said.

"Be there or be square!" Wilmot said, and giving Terry a big thumbs-up, he went to make his phone calls.

Terry watched him go.

"I hope this is going to work," he thought. "I don't feel so sure now. The trouble with Wilmot is he can be a bit headstrong sometimes. He's not what you'd call steady, is Wilmot. I just hope I can rely on him to deliver the goods."

By the time that Amber, Edith, Martin and Wilmot had all turned up for the band photograph on Saturday afternoon, Mr Tanner had already gone to the football and was not there to be asked about his Polaroid camera.

On the assumption that "it would probably be all right, I should think," and that "old Dad wouldn't mind us using a bit of film," Terry sent Wilmot off to take the camera out of the cupboard where it was kept.

"Did your father say you could use that camera?" Mrs Tanner asked, as Wilmot passed through the kitchen with something lumpy and camera-shaped up his jumper.

"Camera?" he said. "What camera's that, Mum? Oh, you mean *this* camera? The one I'm carrying up my jumper for safekeeping so as to protect it from dust? I'm just getting it for Terry. It's for a publicity shot for the band."

"Oh. Well, as long as you've got permission to use it."

"Yes, Mum. Of course. Terry said it would be fine."

"Yes but—" Wilmot's mother began. But he was already out of the door and didn't hear the rest of her sentence. "—I'm not sure that was quite what I meant."

It was decided – for publicity purposes – to seek out unusual and eye-catching locations and back-drops against which the band could be photo-graphed.

"Let's go down to the old slaughter house first," Terry said. "Where they used to kill the pigs. I'll take a few snaps of you down there."

"Yeah, and then maybe the gas works," Wilmot suggested.

"Yeah," Martin agreed. "Or the car breaker's yard. That'd be good. Or how about one of us standing outside of the garbage incinerator down at the tip?"

Amber Watts and Silent Edith didn't seem too keen on these suggestions however.

"I want to be photographed in a meadow of flowers," Amber said.

"What do you want to be photographed in a meadow for?" Wilmot said. "You're not a horse, are you?"

"Well why do you want to be photographed by

the gas works? You're not a bag of wind, are you?" Amber replied. "Though then again—"

Silent Edith whispered a suggestion to Amber which she relayed to the others.

"Edith's suggesting that we have some photographs taken down by the seaside, staring moodily out to sea, just like in poems and stuff, as if we were all dead sad."

"What, you mean as if they'd run out of ice creams?" Wilmot asked. "That sort of sad?"

"Don't be stupid," Amber snapped. "She means as if your heart had been broken and you'd lost your only true love."

"Ice cream is my only true love though," Wilmot, quite reasonably, said. "Not counting dairy milk chocolate of course."

"No, no," Terry said. "Look, we don't want any of that soppy seaside broken-hearted stuff, Amber. We're not that kind of band. We want gritty urban realism and slums and things like real live dog's droppings and sort of squashed hedgehogs in the road and all these buildings with broken windows. That's the sort of photos pop groups have. You need a bit of, you know, credibility."

"How about a picture of us all each holding a

little fluffy kitten?" Amber suggested. "That'd be nice."

The three boys groaned loudly.

"Fluffy kittens," Martin said, "I don't believe it. She's gone mental."

But Amber and Edith held a brief and whispered conference and decided to make a stand.

"If there aren't going to be any little fluffy kittens in it with flowers in meadows and staring out to sea as if you've got a broken heart, we're not doing it and we're going home."

Terry flipped his lid.

"Amber Watts!" he said. "We have not got any kittens! Let alone white fluffy ones. All we have is a big fat cat who lives up the chimney! And there are no flowers in the meadows at this time of year and we live a good fifteen miles away from the sea!"

"We don't care," Amber said. "It's what we want or we're not being in any photos at all."

At length, a compromise was reached. Half of the publicity photos were to be taken as Amber and Edith wanted, and the other half as Terry, Martin and Wilmot wished.

Amber and Edith's photographs would be taken

first, so they all walked down to the local playing fields, which were the nearest thing to a meadow they had. They couldn't find any kittens, but Amber spotted a large Tom cat, which she and Edith managed to get hold off, and they held two paws each, and Terry got a good photograph of it scratching them.

They all went to the hospital then, so that Edith and Amber could get tetanus injections, and then moved on to the canal, which was the nearest thing they had to the sea. Edith and Amber and Wilmot and Martin were photographed staring moodily out along the canal, as if they all had broken hearts and had lost their true loves quite recently and were all dead sad.

Unfortunately, just as Terry took the photograph, a fat man in a rowing boat came into the picture, which rather spoiled the effect, especially as he had a friend with him who was holding up a bucket of maggots while he looked for a nice juicy one with which to bait his fish hook. But as Terry was getting low on film by then, he was unable to take another shot, and they all moved on to the council tip for some shots of gritty realism.

Wilmot and Martin – and a somewhat

uncooperative Amber and Edith – posed alongside a big heap of garden rubbish and old washing machines, trying to look moody and mean.

"Suck your cheeks in, Amber," Terry instructed. "Your face doesn't look thin enough."

"Shut your face up, Terry Tanner," Amber said. "Your lip doesn't look fat enough – and I'll do something about it if you're not careful."

"Try and look like you come from deprived backgrounds and broken homes," Terry said. "Let's get some real suffering into this. Let's see some pain in those eyes."

"I'm desperate for the loo, Terry," Wilmot said, trying to stand still. "Can you get a move on."

"That's it, Wilmot!" Terry said, as Wilmot squirmed in anguish. "That's just the expression I want."

Terry used up the rest of the film down by the back of the fish market, where he got some very interesting shots of the band leaning against a wheelie bin full of old fish guts and crabs' legs. A large seagull came and perched on Wilmot's head, just as Terry's finger pressed the shutter, which – to Terry's mind – made it the best shot of all, though Wilmot wasn't so keen.

* * *

They all went round to Silent Edith's house then, where they had milk and biscuits and argued over which of the Polaroid photographs was the best, and which one should be sent in to the Battle of the Bands for publicity.

Wilmot didn't take much part in the early stages of the discussion, as Silent Edith's mum had let him go upstairs to the bathroom to wash his hair so as to try and get the seagull droppings out of it.

It became clear that they were never going to agree on which photograph to select, so Terry said that as he was the manager, he would make the decision himself, and the others agreed that it should be left up to him to avoid further arguing.

They all went home then (apart from Silent Edith, of course, who already was at home) after agreeing to meet during the week for final rehearsals and for discussions on presentation and on what to wear for the big day when the Battle of the Bands finally took place.

When Wilmot and Terry got back, Wilmot went to watch The Simpsons on TV (Bart Simpson was a kind of hero of his) and Terry went up to his room to decide on the photograph and to draw up a few more water-tight contracts.

After much soul-searching, Terry decided that none of the photographs projected the right image of Boyz 'N Girlz (with zeds). He began thumbing through some magazines he had, and as he turned the pages of an old Nature and Wildlife magazine he suddenly saw just the kind of thing he wanted. He reached into his desk drawer and got out a pair of scissors. A few moments later he called out to his mother that he was just nipping out to post a letter. She told him not to be long as tea was almost ready.

Mr Tanner returned from the football match in a grim and downcast mood.

"We lost again," he said. "Eight nil. Even the ref was crying."

He went up to the bedroom then to have a look for his Polaroid camera. The Tanner family had been invited to a christening the next day and he wanted to make sure that he still had a full roll of film in the camera.

Unfortunately, when he did find his camera, it was to discover that there was not a single exposure left.

"Terry!" he yelled. "Wilmot! Does either of you

two know anything about my film and my camera?"

"Why's that, Dad?" Wilmot called up from the living room. "Have you forgotten how to work it?"

Shortly after The Simpsons had finished on TV, Mr Tanner explained to Wilmot and to Terry that there was now little hope of them receiving any more pocket money until approximately the year 3017.

"That's not so good then, is it, Dad?" Wilmot said sadly.

"No," his father agreed. "It isn't."

13

One-Stringed Guitar

Wilmot was in two minds. But that was not unusual. Wilmot was often in two minds. Sometimes he was in three minds, maybe even four. Sometimes he was in more minds than he really knew how to count. It was amazing how many minds a person could be in when it came to making decisions.

The problem was he didn't know whether to tell his mum and dad about the Battle of the Bands or not. Both he and Terry had so far avoided saying anything directly about their being selected to appear at the Winter Gardens Pavilion on the following Saturday afternoon. They both had a feeling that some things were best kept quiet. Plainly, being selected to take part in such an occasion was a matter of great family pride, and yet—

And yet.

"You know, Wilmot," Terry said. "I think it might be best if we didn't mention anything about it until after we've won."

"Yeah," Wilmot said. "Oddly enough, Terry, I agree with you for once. I don't know why – I just have a gut feeling, in me guts."

"Yeah, well, of course you're well known for your gut feelings, Wilmot. Your guts are famous throughout the town."

"Yeah, not quite as famous as your socks though, are they, Terry? Your socks are enough to make milk curdle."

It was only a token exchange of insults however; neither Wilmot nor Terry really had their hearts in it. It was more for appearances' sake than anything.

"We'll just say we're going out down the park or something," Wilmot said. "Or round to Martin's house."

"Yeah," Terry agreed. "That might be best. Once we've won, it'll be different. They won't mind once we've won."

"No," Wilmot agreed. "They'll be dead proud of us once we've won. We might even get our pocket money back."

"Yeah," Terry said. "Might do."

Three more practices were held during the week.

By Thursday evening, the band were as note perfect as they were ever likely to get.

"We don't want to over-rehearse," Terry said, "Any more than sports athletes want to over-train. Time to ease off now. The only thing we have to sort out now is what are you going to wear on Saturday?"

"I'm going to wear my frilly skirt with all the petticoats," Amber Watts said, "and my gingham top, and I'm going to have my hair in bunches and wear my red shoes, and Edith's going to wear her blue satin dress with her pink leggings and she's going to have a big bow in her hair. What are you going to wear?"

"I think I'm going to shoot myself," Wilmot said, "and wear a big wooden box."

"To be honest, Amber," Terry said. "All that stuff sounds a bit formal to me. It doesn't sound like rock and roll. Haven't you got a pair of leather trousers or something?"

"My dad's got a shammy leather he polishes the car with," Amber said.

"Can't you wear that then?" Wilmot suggested.

"It's a bit small," Amber said. "But I'll see what I can do."

They agreed to wear the trendiest clothes they had and arranged to meet outside of the Winter

Gardens at three pm. On Saturday. Terry had been sent a running order for the contest, and Boyz 'N Girlz (with zeds) were down to play at about four o'clock – in fact they were last on the list.

"That's good," Terry said. "It's better than going on first. If you're last on, you'll be able to make the biggest impact and the judges are bound to remember you. Okay. We'll meet there at three on Saturday. See you then."

On Saturday morning, Wilmot began to feel nervous. It wasn't just the thought of appearing in front of several hundred people, he was also uncertain about what to wear and as to whether his hair style was trendy enough.

"I wish I had a pair of leather trousers, Terry," he said. "Or jeans with big rips in them. That's dead trendy too. And I don't think my hair's right. I look too ordinary, that's my trouble."

"Well, why don't you just rip your jeans yourself then?" Terry suggested.

"I don't think Mum would like that."

"You could always dye your hair then," Terry said.

"Dye my hair!" Wilmot said. "You're joking. Mum would kill me!"

"I don't mean permanently," Terry said. "I mean one of those spray-on dyes, the ones that wash out, the fun ones. We had a can once for Hallowe'en, remember? We sprayed our hair red and went round frightening people and then it all washed out in the bath."

"Oh yeah, that's right," Wilmot said. "Was there any left?"

Terry tried to remember.

"I think so," he said. "I think I left a can of it in the garage. You might find it if you have a look. It's up on the shelf there, just above where Dad keeps his paints."

"Oh, right," Wilmot said. "I'll go and have a look."

At two thirty, Wilmot and Terry left the house and strolled on down towards the Pavilion. Terry – wishing to look the part of a proper agent – had borrowed one of his dad's ties and his double-breasted navy-blue jacket. It was far too large for him, but he carried it off with a certain aplomb. His dad had gone to the football again and so although he hadn't said Terry could borrow his tie and jacket, he hadn't said he couldn't either.

"I ought to have a cigar, really," Terry said. "That's

what agents and managers do."

"Smoking's bad for you," Wilmot reminded him.

"I don't want to smoke it, I just want to wave it about," Terry said. "I'll just nip into the newsagents here and get a bit of licorice."

He left Wilmot on the pavement and soon returned with a fat piece of licorice, which he pretended to "smoke" as they walked along.

"Cool, eh?" he said to Wilmot.

"Never seen anything quite like it," Wilmot told him. He checked in his pocket to see that he had his comb and a spare sheet of tissue paper. In the pocket of his jacket he also had the aerosol of red hair dye which he had found in the garage.

"Do you think they'll give us a dressing room?" he said to Terry.

"Ought to be something," Terry said. "Come on, I can see the others."

Waiting outside the Pavilion were Amber and Edith. Both had decided to abandon the petticoat look and they were wearing tops and leggings and didn't look too bad at all "for girls", as Wilmot said.

Amber had braided her hair and Edith had managed to get hers into dreadlocks and had woven in a few coloured beads for good measure. Martin was standing next to them, all dressed in black as if off to a funeral. He had quite a mournful expression on his face too.

"There's good news and there's bad news," he said.

"Oh no!" Wilmot exclaimed. "You've broken another string."

"Two," Martin said. "I think I must have over tightened them."

"So how many strings have you got left?" Terry demanded.

"One," Martin said.

"One! One string? A one stringed guitar!"

"Sorry," Martin said. "I couldn't help it."

"All right," Terry said, "the rest of you'll just have to play louder, that's all. And so what's the good news?"

"I've still got my potato," Martin said. "No worries there."

"Come on," Terry said. "Let's go and get ready."

Terry led the way round to the side of the Pavilion to the stage door. He showed the man there the pass he had been sent by MegaMix Music.

"Boyz 'N Girlz," Terry announced.

"What, with esses?" the doorman asked.

"No. With zeds."

The doorman waved them through.

"You don't look much like your photograph," he said with a rude laugh. "Dressing room down at the end on the right."

Terry led the band on along the corridor.

"What's he mean we don't look much like our photograph?" Wilmot said. "How can we not look—"

And then he stopped. Because there up on the wall was a publicity shot of all the Battle of the Bands contestants, and under the name Boyz 'N Girlz was a photograph of four gorillas.

"What the—"

"Terry!"

"What's this?"

"Terry Tanner!" Amber said. "What's the big idea?"

But Terry didn't turn a hair.

"I thought it would be a good gimmick," he said. "You know, making out you were gorillas. I didn't think any of those photos were any good. The gorillas looked much better. Come on, let's find the dressing room."

14

Hair-Raising

The dressing room was a large communal one and it was full of people getting changed and ready for their shot at stardom.

When Terry pushed the door open and led the band in, an odd silence settled over the room and the people (mostly teenagers) stared at them with disbelief.

Terry, however, was not phased at all.

"Boyz 'N Girlz," he said. "With zeds. Excuse us, can we sit down over here." And he waved his piece of licorice about in a grand manner and led the way to a clear bench at the far end of the room.

From a distance there was the sound of a jangling electric guitar. The Battle of the Bands was already well underway and another act was launching into their number.

"Young, aren't they?" Wilmot heard someone say. He felt that they were talking about him and the rest of the band.

"Yeah. But then so were the Jackson Five. That was where Michael Jackson started off."

"They're pretty good, some of these kids' bands."

"Yeah—"

And Wilmot realised that the other bands in the room weren't staring at them with amusement, more with respect, and concern – even worry.

"We're in with a chance here," he thought. "We're going to win."

After ten minutes or so, as the bands were gradually called to the stage, a man in a green suit with three earrings in his ears – one in his nose and two in his lip – wandered into the dressing-room and looking around.

"Is Terry Tanner here?" he called out. "Of Tanner Management? The guy who's looking after Boyz 'N Girlz."

For a moment there was silence. Wilmot felt himself colour; he looked at Terry, who had gone deathly pale and seemed to have lost the power of speech.

"Terry," Wilmot hissed. "Say something. You're the manager, aren't you?" And he kicked Terry hard on the ankle, which seemed to bring him back to life.

"Over here, man," Terry said, trying to sound cool and waving his bit of licorice around in what he thought was an agent-like manner. "That's me."

The man in the green suit stared at him. He seemed to have lost the use of his tongue. But eventually, he too got it back. He crossed over and shook Terry by the hand.

"Yeah, man," he said. "Well, man, I'm like, from MegaMix Records, man. Just wanted to say, like, well, hi, man. Great demo, man. So this is the band, eh?" he continued, eyeing Wilmot, Martin, Amber and Silent Edith as if they had just escaped from a reformatory for wayward children. "I didn't like, realise, man, that you were all so, like, well, sort of young, man."

Terry swallowed.

"Oh, yeah, man," he said – trying to get the hang of show-business speak – "we're all like dead young man. It's like dead groovy, man. And fab. Amongst other things. Yeah. Hang loose. Gimme five. Or maybe not. As the case may be."

"Yeah, well, just wanted to say hello, man," the man in the green suit said, "and to say we're looking forward to seeing the band live. Right. Yeah. Well, hang loose, man."

"Hang tight," Wilmot chipped in, feeling he wasn't getting his share of attention. "I'm on lead vocals and comb and tissue paper, man," he said.

"Crazy, man," the green-suited one said, moving towards the door.

"Mad, man," Wilmot agreed. "Totally bonkers."

The green suit disappeared the way it had come, out into the corridor.

"He seemed like a decent sort of bloke," Wilmot said, "even if he did have a lot of earrings."

"I think I'll get a glass of water," Terry said, heading towards the gents toilet.

"I'll come with you," Wilmot said. "It's time I did my hair."

Wilmot and Terry left the dressing room and went to the gents. Terry found a drinking fountain in one corner, while Wilmot went to the mirror and took out the aerosol of red, wash-out fun hair dye, which he had brought from the garage. The label had peeled off it, because the garage was rather damp, but he recognised the tin from when he and Terry had used it before.

"Hurry up, Wilmot," Terry said. "You'll be on any minute."

"Got to get my hair right," Wilmot told him. "Like you said, you need to have a gimmick."

He shook up the aerosol and then sprayed a generous amount of bright red hair colouring on to his head. He looked at the effect in the mirror.

"How's that, Terry?" he asked. "Groovy, eh, or what?"

But Terry didn't answer immediately. He seemed rather preoccupied. He was sniffing the air as if there was an odd, peculiar smell – a smell which he almost recognised but could not immediately identify.

Whoooooosh!

Another long blast from the aerosol shot out on to Wilmot's head.

"Hey, this is a gas all right, eh, Terry? I'm really getting into this," Wilmot said, and he slicked his now bright red hair up into spikes with his comb.

"Er, Wilmot—" Terry said, his nose still twitching.

"Yeah? It's a fantastic hairstyle, isn't it, Terry? Or what? I reckon we're going to win this Battle of the Bands on my hairstyle alone!"

"Wilmot," Terry began, "before you spray any more of that stuff on to—"

Whoooooosh!

He was already too late. Another blast of vivid red hit the Wilmot scalp.

"Wilmot—"

"What?"

"Are you sure that's the hair dye you've got there?"

"Yeah, of course it is. What else would it be? Why're you asking?"

"Which shelf in the garage did you get it from, Wilmot? The top shelf or the middle one?"

"The middle one of course. That was where you said you'd left it."

"No, I d-didn't, Wilmot," Terry stuttered, "not the middle shelf. I said the top. The middle shelf is where Dad—"

"Where Dad *what*?" Wilmot demanded, feeling that he wasn't going to like this.

"It's where Dad keeps – his car paints."

"His *what* paints!" Wilmot almost screamed.

"Car paints, Wilmot. For touching up the scratches on the car. I don't think that's fun hair colouring you've just sprayed your head with there, Wilmot – by the smell of it, that's car paint."

Wilmot turned a deathly shade of pale. The redness of his hair accentuated the pallor of his skin.

He looked like something out of Comic Relief. Yes, he looked like a white-faced clown with a big plastic red nose. Only the nose wasn't on his nose. The nose was on his head. And it had big sticky-up bits which were already beginning to go hard and starting to set like metal spikes.

Wilmot looked from the mirror to his brother and back. Even Terry wasn't laughing. When their mother saw what Wilmot had done to his head! She'd kill Wilmot for doing it, and then she'd kill Terry for not stopping him.

"Terry," Wilmot croaked, "I'm a dead man."

"Don't worry," Terry said, genuinely trying to comfort him. "Don't worry, Wilmot. It'll all come out in the wash."

"Will it?" Wilmot said hopefully.

"No," Terry admitted. "Not if it's car paint. It won't come out at all."

"I'm a double dead man," Wilmot said. "As soon as I'm dead she'll dig me up and kill me all over again. She might even kill me every day for the rest of my life. What am I going to do?!"

But before Terry could answer, a voice came over the back stage intercom.

"Will the members of the band Boyz 'N Girlz –

which I believe is spelt with zeds – please take their instruments and make their way to the east wing of the stage. They're on in five minutes. Repeat, five minute call for Boyz'N Girlz. With zeds."

Wilmot didn't seem to have heard. He just stood there, staring at the red-headed boy in the mirror, the one with the very shiny hair, the one who looked a bit like a psychedelic post box.

"Wilmot!"

He still didn't hear.

"Wilmot! That was the call for the band. You're on. On in five minutes, Come on!"

"My hair!" Wilmot said. "Where am I? Where's Wilmot! Where have I gone? I've lost myself, Terry. I've turned into a red-headed zombie. I'm Wilmot from outer space. The intergalactic post box."

"Wilmot!" Terry said, and he gave him a good shake. "Come to your senses. This is no time to have a nervous breakdown! This is it. Your big chance for stardom. Come on. The others will be waiting. Put your hair out of your mind. You look great. Worry about Mum later. Come on. Let's go! Forget about your head."

"Forget about it!" Wilmot squealed. "I wish I

could. I wish I could saw it off and carry it round in a bag!"

"Wilmot! The £50, remember? The recording contract. Being a heart-throb and Number One in the charts. Don't quit now."

Wilmot's eyes swam back into focus.

"You're right, Terry," he said. "The show must go on."

"That's it, Wilmot," Terry agreed. "Come on, let's go back to the dressing room and get the others."

"Okay," Wilmot said, determination in his voice. "Let's do it, Terry. Let's win the Battle of the Bands."

"That's it, Wilmot. You can always kill yourself afterwards, soon as we've got the prize money."

"Yeah," said Wilmot. "I will."

"Here," Terry said, "have a bite of my licorice."

"Ta," said Wilmot. "You're a pal, Terry. You didn't let me down in my darkest hour. You were there when I needed you."

"You know me, Wilmot," Terry said. "I'm always looking out for you, always thinking of my little brother. Your interests, Wilmot, are always nearest to my heart."

"Come on then." said Wilmot. "Let's go. You know,

Terry," he said as they got to the door, "I think I may have misjudged you."

"It's possible," Terry nodded. "We can't altogether rule it out."

They returned to the dressing round to find Martin, Edith and Amber standing impatiently waiting for them.

"Where've you been, Wilmot Tanner?" Amber demanded. "They've called us to go up to the stage. We're on in a couple of minutes and—" then her mouth dropped wide open. "And what have you done to your hair!"

"Hey," Martin said, "that's fantastic that is Wilmot. You look dead groovy. We'll win this on your barnet alone."

"He looks like an alien!" Amber protested. "Look at him! What colour do you call that!"

"It's called Zingy Metallic Red, if you really want to know," Terry said. "You should see it when the light hits it. It's got little gold flecks in it. It looks dead smart when you see it in the garage."

"What, Wilmot's head?"

"No, our dad's old car."

"But it's so unnatural," Amber went on, "Who

the heck has got hair that colour?"

"You have," Wilmot said.

"I have not!"

"You flipping have, Amber Watts. You look like a flipping traffic light that's permanently on stop."

"Now look here, Wilmot Tan—"

But the voice came over the intercom again.

"Last call for Boyz 'N Girlz. Last call. If they aren't at the stage in two minutes, we'll have to go on to the next act."

"Come on," Terry said. "Grab your stuff and let's go. This is it. Forget about everything else for the next ten minutes. Your big chance for stardom has come!"

15

Gimme Ten, Now and Then

Had his mind not been concerned with other things – such as the thick coating of spray car paint on his head – Wilmot might possibly have been nervous. It was probably quite an unusual thing too, for a budding chart-topper and heart-throb to step out for his first appearance before the public thinking, "My mum's going to kill me when I get home."

But Wilmot's preoccupation worked to his advantage, and when he and Martin and Amber and Edith heard the compere announce, "And our next act is a new band of great talent, able to copy the sound of anyone you care to mention. Will you welcome Boyz 'N Girlz – which I'm reliable informed is spelt with zeds," he stepped out on to the stage without any fear in him at all.

How the other three felt, Wilmot had no idea.

Amber never appeared to be nervous about anything. And anyway, there wasn't that much to be nervous about.

The Battle of the Bands had not attracted as large a crowd as the organisers had hoped. The place was not even half full, and most of those present were friends or relatives of the band members taking part in the competition.

Wilmot made his way towards one of the microphones, blinking into the lights. To one corner of the stage he could make out a panel of three judges, there to decide on which band was the best.

From the wings of the stage, Wilmot heard Terry whispering some last words of encouragement.

"Okay! Just imagine you're in the garden shed, and go for it!"

Terry had considered appearing himself with the band to do a drum solo on his biscuit tins, but he had decided against this at the last moment when he found that his lids had disappeared, which would have badly affected the sound.

Silence descended upon the auditorium. Wilmot looked around. Martin was at his left, his one-stringed guitar at the ready, Amber was at his right, her violin tucked under her chin, the bow ready in her hand. Edith was standing just behind him, getting ready to launch into her silent backing vocals.

"Okay," Wilmot said. "A one, a two, a one two three – four!"

And they were off.

"*I love you baby,*" Wilmot sang. "*Don't mean maybe. Gimme five. Snakes alive. Gimme ten. Now and then. Oooeee, oooeee. I'm so free. Feel like a cup of tea.*"

Then he launched into the chorus.

"*Cadgy wadgy woo woo. Cadgy wadgy foo foo. Cadgy wadgy choo choo. Oh baby if I had to choose between you and my trainers it would be a penalty shootout.*"

Then taking up his comb and tissue paper, he launched into his solo while Martin hammered at the last of his guitar strings with his potato. Amber's violin shrieked and screamed and Edith gyrated along, doing her silent backing vocals, and looking more like she was having a fit than ever.

Sweat ran down Wilmot's face. His hair felt very strange. Sort of tight and pointy, and very solid. He launched into the second verse.

"*Don't be late,*" he sang. "*You're my milkshake. Pass me the football. Let me buy you a burger, baby, down at*

McDonald's. And you can pay for the cokes." And then he was away into the chorus again.

"*Cadgy wadgy woo woo, cadgy wadgy foo foo. Cadgy wadgy choo choo, oh baby if I had to choose between you and my trainers it would be a penalty shootout.*"

He sang the chorus once more, did another few bars on the comb and tissue paper, and then they were into the big finish and the song ended on a high note, followed by a loud resounding twang as the last of Martin's guitar strings broke in two and as the potato he was strumming it with shot out of his hand, bounced off the stage, and landed in the audience.

There was silence.

Complete, utter, total silence.

Yet it wasn't the silence of disapproval or dislike. It was more the silence of incomprehension, it was the silence of the stunned and bewildered. It was the silence of those whose minds cannot fully take in what their eyes have just seen and their ears have just heard.

But then the sound of clapping and whistling came from the wings.

"Great!" Terry shouted. "Fantastic! Brilliant!"

His clapping was picked up by the audience, and

they gave the band a polite – if subdued – round of applause.

The four band members bowed towards the audience and the judges, and they left the stage as the compere rushed on. He took the microphone.

"Boyz 'N Girlz, ladies and gentlemen!" he said. "A very original act. You can't say we don't have variety here at the Battle of the Bands. A big hand now for our next contestants, Snoop Scroggy and the Porridge Bashers."

Another band strolled on to the stage as Wilmot and co. left it. Wilmot got another glimpse of himself in a mirror as they returned to the dressing room.

"She's going to kill me," he thought, "she is definitely going to kill me."

Amber put her violin back into its case.

"What do you think then?" Martin asked. "Reckon we've won?"

Amber looked at him with disdain. "Won? Us? You must be joking. Still, it was a good laugh for a while, wasn't it. Are you coming then, Edith? I don't think I'm hanging about here."

Edith nodded and the two girls headed for the door.

"But aren't you staying?" Terry said. "For the results?"

"Not much point, is there?" Amber said. "That was an absolutely terrible racket, that was. The only decent thing in this group is the violin playing and the silent backing vocals. The rest is just rubbish and the song was even worse. So we're off."

"You can't just go!" Terry yelled. "You signed a contract with me. You owe me half of all your earnings!"

"But we haven't earned anything," Amber reasonably pointed out. "All we've made so far is one big nothing."

"Well, I want half of that then," Terry said.

"You can have it all," Amber told him. "Come along, Edith," she said to her friend. "Let us leave these tone deaf idiots to their fantasies and dreams. I fear they are nothing but stupid boys who have no sense at all and nothing but space between their ears. They will never be pop stars, they will only ever be stupid Wallies. Come, let us depart. We shall seek stardom elsewhere, far away from this bunch of losers."

And with that Amber and Edith flounced out of the dressing room without so much as a backward glance.

Terry, Wilmot and Martin watched them go.

"Just ignore them," Terry said. "Bands are always splitting up due to musical differences. We can easily replace them. They're only girls. We'll get a couple of dummies or something. It's not a problem."

"Do you think we've won then, Terry?" Wilmot asked.

But Terry seemed not to have heard him and he engrossed himself in smoking what was left of his licorice.

"I said do you think we've won then, Terry?"

But then Terry developed a coughing fit.

"I said—"

But then the voice came over the intercom again.

"All bands back to the stage now to hear the judges' decision. All bands—"

"Well," Terry said. "We'll soon find out."

16

Kneecaps for Cricket Balls

It had started to rain. Not heavily though. It was just one of those dismal drizzles, the kind that gets right down the back of your neck and somehow worms its way up your sleeves.

Martin, Wilmot and Terry walked despondently along through the grey, wet streets. They had left as soon as the result was announced. They hadn't stayed for the rest. The Battle of the Bands had been won by an all-girl group called Little Misses Molly, all of whom were accomplished musicians, singers and dancers, and who had delighted the judges with their original number entitled Shaka Maka Booty (Get Down To It, Hot Rhubarb). They had won the recording contract and the first prize.

Wilmot looked at his reflection as they passed a shop window. His red, gloss-painted hair was unaffected by the rain, and it still stuck up in all directions.

"I look like Sonic the Hedgehog," he thought. "She's going to kill me, she really is."

They came to a corner and a parting of the ways.

"I'd best be getting home then," Martin said. "Sorry we didn't win, Wilmot, after all that work and stuff. And sorry about all my guitar strings breaking."

"Don't worry," Terry said. "It sounds better when you play it like that."

But Martin didn't seem to hear.

"See you Monday," he said.

"See you, Martin," Wilmot said despondently, "if I'm still alive."

"What? Oh yeah. Good luck with your hair, Wilmot. I'm sure your mum won't really mind."

"You reckon?"

"No, you're right. She's going to kill you, Wilmot. See you at the funeral then."

"Cheers, Martin. Bye."

Martin went his way, Terry and Wilmot went theirs. Neither of them spoke for a while, but Wilmot kept glancing at Terry as if he had something to say. Finally he came out with it.

"Terry—"

"Yes, Wilmot?"

"You know at the end of the Battle of the Bands, when they announced the prize money—"

"Yeah?"

"They said it was £5,000."

"Yeah?"

"You told me it was £50."

"Did I?"

"Yeah. And all the letters and the newspaper ad and everything, they all said £50 too."

"Did they? That's odd, isn't it, Wilmot."

"And the other funny thing is that the newspaper ad and one of those letters, they both had Tipp-ex on them."

"Did they? That was strange, wasn't it, Wilmot."

"I wonder how that happened, Terry."

"Yeah, me too."

"And then there was that other letter, with all the spelling and typing mistakes. That was a bit odd as well. So odd, it could almost have been a forgery, eh?"

"Do you think so, Wilmot? Do you really think such a thing is possible. Who would stoop so low as to do a thing like that?"

There was a long pause.

"It was you, wasn't it, Terry," Wilmot said.

"Me?" Terry asked. "In what way, Wilmot? How do you mean?"

"You. You tried to con me. You did the Tipp-exing! And you rewrote that letter on dad's computer. You knew the prize was £5,000 all along. But you made out it was £50. And if we'd won, you'd have kept the money and only given us £25 for the four of us – and you'd still have taken commission, wouldn't you!"

Terry turned to face Wilmot, his expression one of wounded innocence.

"How can you think such a thing, Wilmot. How can you think so little of your own brother. To imagine that I'd ever pull a stunt like that. How can you even think it!"

"Because it's what you're like, Terry," Wilmot said. "And you tried to rip me off on those contracts too, didn't you! You're a shifty, sleazy, money-grabbing toad, you are. And when we get home, I'm going to ram the insides of an old toilet roll right up your nostril and then I'm going to use your kneecaps for cricket balls."

"Oh are you just!" Terry said. "Well in that case I'm going to Boo-Jitsu you, Wilmot. I'm going to Boo you so hard in the Jitsus that you'll be able to use your tongue for a scarf!"

"Oh are you now. Well in that case—"

But Wilmot stopped in mid-threat. They were at the garden gate. There was their house. There was the happy home he had once known. There was his dad, back from the football, out in the garden, looking pleased, as if his team had won.

And there was his mother, standing talking to his dad, the two of them laughing about something, sharing a joke, looking as if they loved each other and that everything in the garden was rosy, even the geraniums.

Wilmot opened the gate. He and Terry walked through. The gate banged shut behind them. His mum looked up at the sound. She saw her two sons.

"Hi, Wilmot! Hi, Terry! Tea won't be long."

She looked away. She was still smiling. Then her head stopped moving. It seemed to freeze on her shoulders. It slowly moved back for another look.

The next thing Wilmot saw was that her eyes were bulging. Then her jaw was dropping open. Her arm was moving. Her finger was pointing. A gurgle was coming from her throat.

"Hello, Mum," Wilmot said. "Do you like my new hairstyle?"

And it was round about then that the screaming started.

17

Short Back and Sides

"*Why*, Wilmot. That's what I just don't understand. *Why*?"

"It was an accident, Mum," Wilmot told her for the umpty-ninth time. "I thought it was the wash-out hair dye. The fun stuff."

"But didn't you *realise*! Didn't you *smell* it. Didn't you *think*? And what were you doing dying your hair anyway?!"

"I was going to be pop star, Mum. It's a long story."

"Okay, okay. Let's try some more shampoo. Let's just try and wash it out and we'll say no more about it."

Only saying no more about it didn't seem to work. Because no sooner had Wilmot's mum said, "We'll say no more about it," than she would give him one of those terrible looks and then she'd start sighing again, and within a couple of seconds she'd be asking,

"*Why*, Wilmot. But *why*?"

But Wilmot didn't really seem to know.

It wasn't just saying no more about it that didn't seem to work. Shampooing it didn't seem to work either. After using several bottles of the stuff, Mrs Tanner gave up.

"Come on, Wilmot, get your coat," she said. "We're going to Mr Emerson."

And she dragged him off to the barber's.

Mr Emerson was one of those old fashioned barbers, the kind who have no hair.

"Not much of an advertisement for getting your hair cut, is he?" Wilmot whispered to his mother, as they sat waiting to be attended to. But she just shushed him quiet, and dabbed at her eyes with her tissue, and then she gave him one of her said, heartbroken looks again, and she said,

"But *why*, Wilmot? *Why*?"

But he still didn't seem to know.

Mr Emerson sat Wilmot in the adjustable chair, raised it to the right height, and sized up the job.

He'd seen it all before. Hair with paint in it, hair

with glue in it, hair with birds' nests in it. He was unflappable.

"Short back and sides, is it?" he asked Mrs Tanner.

"Very short," she nodded, "very back, and very sides as well."

Mr Emerson picked up his scissors.

"And I take it you do want all the red bits cut out?"

"I think so," Mrs Tanner said. "I think so, yes."

By the time Mr Emerson had finished, Wilmot felt very chilly around the ears and he looked as though he had just been signed up for the army in the real SAS. He stared at the crew-cut head in the mirror. Was it him? Was it the genuine Wilmot? He supposed it was. Or it would be again, one day, when his hair had all grown back.

Mr Emerson held a hand mirror up so that Wilmot could see the back of his neck.

"Okay?"

"I suppose so."

"Anything on it?" Mr Emerson asked.

"How about a wig?" Wilmot suggested.

"I don't think so, thank you," Mrs Tanner said. "We've had quite enough *on* it already!"

* * *

As the days passed, things gradually returned to normal. Wilmot's mum only said, "But *why*, Wilmot, *why*?" about twenty times a day now instead of the usual sixty. And whenever she saw Terry she still said, "But why didn't you *stop* him, Terry, *why*?" but she was trying to cut down on that too.

Several years pocket money had been lost – needless to say – as a result of the car paint on the head incident, and Wilmot had worked out that he was unlikely to receive any more pocket money until he was five hundred and ten years old.

He couldn't claim to be pleased about this, as he had no other source of income, and his mum refused to let him do a paper round as the job would have taken him, "Along by that shop where they sell the car paint," and she wasn't taking any more chances.

The slight unpleasantness at home had temporarily driven thoughts of stardom from Wilmot's mind. But only temporarily. Whenever he heard the latest hit on the radio or saw the latest pop sensation on TV, he kept thinking to himself, "I'm sure I could do it, if I could just get the breaks. I'm sure I could be number one in the charts."

* * *

When a letter fell on to the doormat a week later therefore, practically landing on Wilmot's toes as he came down for breakfast, a letter franked with the unmistakeable MegaMix Records Inc. logo, Wilmot picked it up with trembling fingers.

Maybe his moment for stardom had come after all.

Wilmot stuffed the letter up his pyjama top and went with it to the bathroom, carefully locking the door behind him.

Because the letter was not addressed to Wilmot. It was addressed to Terry. To Terry Tanner Management Ltd. (Agent To The Stars). But that didn't matter to Wilmot. He was going to steam the letter open.

Now Wilmot knew that this was wrong. He knew that he shouldn't do it. But he justified it to himself on the grounds that Terry had tried to swindle him and had lied to him about the prize money, so he was entitled to take revenge, if only to safeguard his interests.

He turned on the hot tap and let the water run into the sink until steam was rising up. He held the envelope over the steam and gently pulled the envelope open and extracted what was inside.

There was a letter. And something else:

Dear Mr Tanner, the letter read. *I am afraid that you must have been unable to stay for the announcement of all the results at our Battle of the Bands contest on Saturday last. You may not realise that although your band, Boyz 'N Girlz (with Zeds), did not win the Battle, it was however voted first in the Young Talent and Stars of Tomorrow section. Although the live band was nothing like the demo tape you sent in, the judges thought them to be new, fresh, highly original, and just the kind of thing the world of pop needs. The line-up was unique (we especially loved the silent backing vocals – strong visual performance) and it is many years since we have seen a band with its own comb and tissue paper player. We also thought the lead singer to be immensely talented. Not only were we knocked out by his comb and tissue paper solo, his singing was something else, and his hairstyle was out of this world.*

Maybe in a few years, when the band are a little older, you might care to come back to us, and we would be more than happy to listen to them again. In the meantime, please accept the enclosed MegaMix

CD tokens with our compliments. These can be used in any record store for the purchase of CDs, T-shirts or any of our merchandise.

Yours sincerely,

Hiram B. Fireum. Managing Director.

MegaMix Records.

Wilmot shook the envelope then and four gift tokens fluttered to the floor. He picked them up and looked at what was printed on them.

Each of them was worth £50.

£50!

Four £50 tokens. One for Wilmot, one for Martin, one for Amber, one for Edith and one for—

No. That was it. That was all there was. One for every member of the group. Not for anybody else.

The handle of the bathroom door rattled.

"Wilmot!" Terry's voice called. "Are you going to be in there forever?"

"No," Wilmot said. "Be out in a moment."

He replaced everything inside the envelope, hid the envelope inside his pyjamas, let the water out of the sink, and went to open the door.

* * *

After breakfast, Wilmot went up to his room. He took three separate envelopes, put a £50 token into each one, and addressed one to Amber, one to Martin, and one to Silent Edith.

Then he went and got his bottle of Tipp-ex out of the drawer.

Later that morning, as Terry was on his way out to meet up with his friend Dave for a kickabout down at the playing fields, Wilmot stopped him in the corridor and handed him the envelope.

"Letter for you here, Terry," he said.

"When did that get here? That's late."

"Must have fallen under the mat or something. Probably came with this morning's post. Here you are. Look, it's from the record company, I think."

"Is it," Terry said. "Is it? Let me see!"

He hurriedly tore the envelope open, unfolded the letter, then stared at it in total bewilderment.

"What's it say?" Wilmot asked him.

"Nothing," Terry said. "Look!"

He held the letter up for Wilmot to see. All it said was,

Dear Mr Tanner,

Yours sincerely,
Hiram B. Fireum. Managing Director.
MegaMix Records.

Everything else had been Tipp-exed out.

Wilmot handed the sheet of paper back.

"That's a funny letter, isn't it, Terry," he said. "It looks like someone's spilt a bottle of liquid paper on that."

"Yeah but – but – how could that have happened?" Terry said. "You don't just spill Tipp-ex all over a letter like that! Not a proper secretary."

"No, they *can* do it," Wilmot said. "Remember, they did it the last time, when they spilt some Tipp-ex on the letter and accidentally changed £5000 to £50. Do you remember that, Terry? These things can happen."

"Just a minute, Wilmot," Terry said. "Just one flipping minute! You've been at my letter, haven't you?"

"*Me*?" Wilmot said. "What makes you think that."

"Hang on," Terry said. "Hang on."

He took the letter to the window and held it up to the light. There it was, all clearly visible now. All about the prize and the gift tokens—

"Gift tokens?!" Terry yelled. "Where are they, Wilmot! Where's mine?"

"You didn't get one, Terry!" Wilmot said. "You don't get anything for being a greedy, grasping con-artist. All you're going to get is the insides of an old toilet roll! Stuck up a secret place, that only trained SAS men with special haircuts know about!"

"Oh, is that so, now!" Terry said. "Well, let me tell you something, Wilmot you bald-headed twit face! You want to have a Number One hit, do you? Well, you won't be disappointed! Because you'll get a Number One hit, all right, And then you'll get a Number Two hit. And then you'll get a Number Three hit. And then you'll get a boot up your backside as well. And then I'm going to get you round the neck with a secret Boo-Jitsu hold that'll make your eyeballs bulge out like boiled eggs!"

"Oh, will you now! Well, we'll just see about that then, won't we!"

And the two brothers fell on to each other, and began whirling round so fast that it was difficult to tell which was Wilmot and which was Terry. But Mrs Tanner didn't really care which was which, she sent both of them to their rooms and then made them spend the rest of the weekend cleaning out the garage until it was spotless.

"She's cruel to us," Wilmot said, after about three hours of cleaning.

"She is," Terry agreed. "She's the worst mother brothers have ever had."

"We should ring up KidScrape, the child help line," Wilmot said. "And put in a complaint."

"We should," Terry agreed.

"Or run away from home."

"Good idea," Terry said. "We'll do that, soon as we've had some dinner."

"Terry," Wilmot said, after a while, "I'll let you have half of my MegaMix gift token if you like."

"Thanks, Wilmot," Terry said, brightening up. "Will you really? You're a pal. I'm going to share my next pocket money with you, Wilmot. I'm going to split it with you, straight down the middle."

They ran away from home after dinner. They got as far as the garden shed when Terry was taken bad with stomach cramps. Wilmot had to lie him down on the compost bags.

"You go on without me, Wilmot," Terry said bravely. "You escape to freedom. You get away while you can, little brother. I'll stay here and try to fight them off for you."

But Wilmot wasn't to be taken in.

"You're shamming, Terry," he said. "You're just putting it on so's I'll run away from home on my own. And then when I've gone, you'll go into my room and have all my football cards and find my secret store of Smarties. You're sly and sneaky, you are, and I'm going to jam this flower pot on your head to teach you a lesson."

"Oh, are you!" Terry said, scrambling to his feet, his cramp suddenly gone. "Well, I'm going to shove you inside this compost bag, Wilmot. The next time you look in the mirror – you'll be wearing it!"

Mrs Tanner heard the terrible noise coming from the shed and went out to investigate. She found one of her sons with a flowerpot rammed over his head, while the other one seemed to be somehow trapped inside a compost bag – almost wearing it, like a jacket, with his arms poking out of the sides.

"And just what are you two doing *now*!" she demanded.

Wilmot peered at her sheepishly from inside his compost bag coat.

"Nothing really, Mum," he said. "Just running away from home. Aren't we, Ter?" he asked the flower pot.

"Yeah," the flower pot nodded, with a faint echo. "We're running away to a better life and pastures new."

Mrs Tanner looked at them.

"Running away, are you?" she said. "I see. Okay. Wait there, then," she told them. "I'll go and pack your rucksacks."

And she walked out.

"She doesn't really mean it, does she, Terry?" Wilmot said when she had gone. "She doesn't *really* want us to leave home, does she? I mean, she loves us really, doesn't she, Ter? We're her pride and joy."

But Terry didn't seem able to hear him any more.

Maybe he had his flower pot on too tight, and it was stopping his circulation.

"Don't worry, Ter," said Wilmot. "Don't panic. I'll soon get it off you, mate. I won't let you come to any harm."

And he slowly picked up the garden spade.

And then carefully took aim.